W9-BUU-835

Get Your Coventry Romances Home Subscription NOW

And Get These 4 Best-Selling Novels *FREE*:

LACEY
by Claudette Williams

THE ROMANTIC WIDOW
by Mollie Chappell

HELENE
by Leonora Blythe

THE HEARTBREAK TRIANGLE
by Nora Hampton

A Home Subscription! It's the easiest and most convenient way to get every one of the exciting Coventry Romance Novels! ...And you get 4 of them FREE!

You pay nothing extra for this convenience: there are no additional charges...you don't even pay for postage! Fill out and send us the handy coupon now, and we'll send you 4 exciting Coventry Romance novels absolutely FREE!

SEND NO MONEY, GET THESE
FOUR BOOKS FREE!

C1281

MAIL THIS COUPON TODAY TO:
COVENTRY HOME
SUBSCRIPTION SERVICE
6 COMMERCIAL STREET
HICKSVILLE, NEW YORK 11801

YES, please start a Coventry Romance Home Subscription in my name, and send me FREE and without obligation to buy, my 4 Coventry Romances. If you do not hear from me after I have examined my 4 FREE books, please send me the 6 new Coventry Romances each month as soon as they come off the presses. I understand that I will be billed only $9.00 for all 6 books. There are no shipping and handling nor any other hidden charges. There is no minimum number of monthly purchases that I have to make. In fact, I can cancel my subscription at any time. The first 4 FREE books are mine to keep as a gift, even if I do not buy any additional books.

For added convenience, your monthly subscription may be charged automatically to your credit card.

☐ Master Charge   ☐ Visa
42101   **42101**

Credit Card # _____

Expiration Date _____

Name _____
(Please Print)

Address _____

City _____ State _____ Zip _____

Signature _____

☐ Bill Me Direct Each Month **40105**

Publisher reserves the right to substitute alternate FREE books. Sales tax collected where required by law. Offer valid for new members only.
Allow 3-4 weeks for delivery. Prices subject to change without notice.

THE
HEIRESS
COMPANION

by

Madeleine Robins

FAWCETT COVENTRY • NEW YORK

THE HEIRESS COMPANION

Published by Fawcett Coventry Books, a unit of CBS Publications, the Consumer Publishing Division of CBS Inc.

Copyright © 1981 by Madeleine Robins

All Rights Reserved

ISBN: 0-449-50228-7

Printed in the United States of America

First Fawcett Coventry printing: December 1981

10   9   8   7   6   5   4   3   2   1

for my Grandmother,
Louise Small George (1894–1980),
who lived the part of the "princess"

Chapter 1

"Excuse me, miss, but if you could step into the small saloon for a moment?" The butler's diffident voice broke into Miss Cherwood's concentration on the lists and notes before her.

"Someone to see me, Drummey?" she asked, frowning slightly at a bill for wax candles. There were only three persons she knew of who might be desiring an audience with her today, taken up with last minute details for the party as she was. And the thought of breaking off her work to speak with any one of the three did not please her. There was the chance that it might be Mr. Greavesey, the physician's assistant, bringing Lady Bradwell's drops and eyewash. Since Mr. Greavesey showed an alarming and distasteful tendency to moist sighings and significant glances when in Miss Cherwood's vicinity, he would hardly be a welcome visitor. If it was Lady Bradwell's older son he would likely be hot with a brainstorm regarding the stables or one of the shooting pens, and while Lord Bradwell was as good-natured as the day is long, he was also long-winded when enthusiastic, and totally impervious to polite hints that perhaps one might have other things to attend to than a new design for tack pegs.

The only other person who might not realize that the ladies of Broak Hall were not "at home" this afternoon, Miss Cherwood thought with a sniff, was Lady Bradwell's younger son, whose arrival had been expected hourly for the last week. Miss Cherwood had no sympathy for Lyndon Bradwell, having attended his mother during much of her illness six months before and seen how important his arrival was to her mistress. Indeed, the party which was consuming so much was being held at Lady Bradwell's expressed command, to welcome home her prodigal son, gone these six years in the army, and in Naples.

"Gone for six years, and still it takes him six months to return home when his poor mamma is deathly ill! The least That Man could do now is return according to his own schedule." Patting a stray curl briskly into place, Miss Cherwood returned her attention to the butler. "Can-

8

not the gentleman join me here?" she asked, resigning herself to Mr. Greavesey's oily compliments or Lord Bradwell's inarticulate enthusiasms.

"Well, that's the first thing, miss. It isn't a gentleman. It's a young woman, miss, or perhaps I dare say a young lady. And I believe she's arrived by stagecoach. And she insists that she talk directly to you, miss."

"A mystery? Well, thank you, Drummey. I shall join her directly." This *was* strange. There was no young woman she could think of who would be calling at Broak on a chill, raining afternoon, certainly not when the house was known to be under covers for the party preparations; there was absolutely no one who should be arriving by stagecoach and asking particularly to see *her*. Miss Cherwood left the library and made her way to the small saloon.

As she entered the room and her visitor turned to greet her, Miss Cherwood experienced a shock. The face that greeted her, the shade of chestnut hair, even its arrangement, might have been her own mirror image—seven years before. "Margaret!" she cried joyfully, and the two of them flew into an embrace.

"Rowena, you haven't any idea how glad I am to see you!" Margaret Cherwood confessed at last, freed from the confines of spencer and bonnet. "I was afraid you would turn me away at once. Not but what you may, when I tell you what I have done, but O! Renna, it was too much to be borne."

"Why, yes, dear, I imagine it was, if it put you in such a state. Now sit here, and I'll ring for some tea, and you shall tell me all about it." Miss Cherwood guided her cousin to a comfortable chair, coaxed her to settle into it and to accept a shawl for her shoulders, and, having ordered the tea, seated herself opposite on the sofa.

"Now, what brings you to Broak in the middle of such a cold, dreary day? And in the midst of the Season, at that?"

"I vow, Renna, it wasn't my idea at all, but I could not bear the idea of going to my grandmamma Lewis's, and I knew that you were on the way to Bristol—well, in a manner of speaking, anyway. So I left the stage at Reading and bought a ticket to Plymouth, but the coachman let me down almost outside the gates of Broak."

"Which answers my questions nicely, and tells me nothing about why you are here, or why you were traveling to Lady Lewis's. She's not ill, I trust? I find it—forgive me—a trifling bit difficult to believe that your mamma has let you from her sight as easily as that."

"But it was *Mamma's* idea," Miss Margaret informed her cousin. "Mamma says that I am an ungrateful wretch, and don't deserve to bear the name that I do."

If Rowena was supposed to have been shocked by this dire pronouncement, it did not do its work. She crowed with laughter. "Refused an offer she wanted you to accept, did you? Nothing is more calculated to send your mamma into a

10

fit of dejection, Meggy love. I heard just such fustian when I refused an offer from that horrible Sir Jason Slyppe—the fellow with the badly made corset and the spots."

"He's now a *peer*," Margaret informed her cousin glumly. "He loaned the Regent a *scandalous* amount of money. And Mamma does seem to want him in the family."

"Then, begging my uncle's pardon, she had best marry him herself," Rowena said flatly. "And you are being rusticated?"

"I wouldn't mind so much, for I am fond of Grandmamma Lewis, but when I go to visit her she always finds so many ways for me to be useful—"

"A slave," Miss Cherwood suggested succinctly.

"Rowena!" Margaret protested. "It's just that I couldn't face being there all alone, erranding for Grandmamma and being expected to be repentant when I'm not in the least, and—"

"I quite understand, Meg. So you came to me, for which I am flattered. But now—what on earth shall I do with you?"

Margaret looked puzzled. "Do? Renna, I hadn't meant to be a charge on you—"

"Don't be an absurd infant, my dear. It's only that I am differently circumstanced now than I used to be. I think, in fact I am certain that Lady B will be delighted that you have come, but just on the off chance that I cannot keep you with me for more than a few days—you see, love, I'm an employee now, and not a guest, and

Lady Bradwell—well, I do owe her the courtesy of asking her permission before I offer you permanent asylum."

"If it's not convenient—" Margaret began, a little stiffly.

"You'll continue to your grandmamma's? Nonsense, love. You are no trouble at all. You know what a manager I am, and I am only trying to take everything into account so that we cannot be taken down by chance. More particularly, so that Lady B won't be troubled by anything. That is my job here, after all, and she's the dearest old thing, and still a little invalidish."

"I thought all old ladies treated their companions dreadfully?" Margaret announced tentatively.

"Which is what comes, I collect, of reading subscription-library novels. No, Meg, she's a very kind lady, but a little troubled. First she was so sick—her life was despaired of for a time, but she's almost recovered now. And her eyes were left dreadfully weakened by the fever, and she will *not* take proper care unless she's *hounded* to do so, and now she's waiting for her scapegrace son to return from abroad, as he was supposed to do last week."

"Will I be terribly troublesome to you—or her? Ought I to find a position as a companion, or a governess, or something such?" Her tone was not enthusiastic.

"Who would hire a chit just out from the schoolroom, with looks like yours? You'd have

12

every papa and older brother listening to the lessons in the nursery! Trust me, Meggy my dear. You'll probably be of great assistance to me by keeping my lady company while I am so busy. I am caught up in arranging a party we are to have on Friday evening—if Mr. Lyndon Bradwell condescends to make his appearance!"

"Who is that?" Margaret began. A knock on the door at that moment announced Drummey and the tea tray, and Rowena, giving orders for the disposition of Miss Margaret's trunk and bandboxes, now waiting with the gatekeeper at the end of the long drive, did not answer. But when both cousins had their tea and seedcake before them, Margaret asked again, "Who is Lyndon Bradwell?"

"Lady Bradwell's younger son. I am entirely out of temper with the man. Unreasonable, I suppose, but there it is. You see, he went off to the army six years ago, and then, when he sold out his commission—when was it? I have heard this story a thousand times from Lady Bradwell! I think it must have been two years ago—he'd an offer to become part of Sir William A'Court's staff. So he hasn't seen his mamma in all that time. Even last fall, when the poor lady was so dreadfully ill—yes, I'd told you that!—he could not be found, even when Lady Bradwell's greatest wish was to see him. And now, though she is mending, she is still fragile, and easily depressed, and still he delays his arrival. I have found that ridiculous woman rereading his letter—in which, mind you, he *swore* to return by

13

the twenty-first of this month—lying abed and reading that letter in the half dark! I swear I don't know which one of them I would like to shake first. And here it is, almost the end of the month, and still no sign of him. Do you wonder I am out of charity with him?"

"Perhaps he was delayed?" Margaret suggested mildly.

"I promise you I know all the reasonable answers, Meg. I just do hate to see Lady B so turned about by his absence. Now that I haven't Mamma to fuss over, you can see that I've veritably adopted Lady Bradwell. And then there's this party. Thirty couples invited, and we have no idea as to whether or not the guest of honor will be attending! All of which," Rowena finished, "has nothing to do with your predicament. Now listen, Drummey will have moved your boxes into one of the guest rooms. If you would like to change your dress and tidy yourself a bit, I shall go and speak to Lady Bradwell." Margaret smiled apprehensively. "Now, I promise I shall neither send you back to your mamma nor let your grandmother make a scullery girl of you. Even if Lady Bradwell cannot play the hostess for you, I have other resources, I promise you. So go along, now. I'll come to you in a while." She placed Margaret in the hands of a housemaid.

"Rowena, you're wonderful." Margaret smiled mistily over her shoulder.

"Nonsense," Miss Cherwood returned firmly, and returned to the office.

Some fifteen minutes later Rowena entered Lady Bradwell's room to find her employer propped against a mountain of pillows, piles of close-written papers littered across the bed, and her hated blue glass spectacles lying unused at the bottom of the bed. Only a few braces of candles were lit to brighten the rain-dreary room.

"Lady Bradwell, I am shocked at you," she scolded, lighting candles until the room glowed with their light. "This room as dark as the tomb, and still you sit here, ruining your eyes by reading. What the doctor, and Lord Bradwell, your prodigal son will say! And *I* shall be raked over the coals for being so remiss—cast out on my ear, no doubt, and now, too, when I specifically need your help."

Lady Bradwell cheerfully ignored this teasing. "Scold all you like, dear, but do tell me what sort of help *I* can give *you*. If you knew how wretchedly helpless I have felt these months, lying here like the stupidest creature in nature!"

In a few short, highly colored sentences Rowena sketched her cousin's plight. "I should hate to return her to her mother or her grandmother. Her mother—well, I've told you about my Aunt Dorothea, ma'am. And while Lady Lewis can be amusing in an ill-tempered, kind-hearted sort of way, she *is* a tyrant unless one stands up to her. And Meggy just isn't up to her weight."

"Well, my dear, if she is anything like you we

shall be pleased to have her at Broak as long as she cares to stay."

"You are much, much too good." Rowena gave the older woman a careful hug.

"Not at all, child. I imagine I am as amusing and ill tempered as your Margaret's grandmother. For instance, I shall expect to meet this paragon of a cousin at dinner tonight. And I assume she is out, and has an evening dress she can wear to our party."

"She's out, that I know. As for a dress, I'm sure she has one. If not, I can loan her one of mine."

Lady Bradwell regarded her companion ironically. "Your cousin is—um, a statuesque woman, Rowena?"

Miss Cherwood permitted herself a rueful smile. "If you mean, is she a great bean pole like me, ma'am, no she isn't. If you can picture me, at nineteen rather than seven-and-twenty, with my hair in short curls, and less seven inches of height, there you have Margaret."

"I begin to think that I may enjoy myself with your young cousin, Rowena. Does she ever laugh at you?"

"Would she dare? I could crush her with a look, and she's not got your presence, ma'am," Rowena replied delightedly, cheered by her mistress's good spirits.

"You mean my bad-temperedness," Lady Bradwell corrected sweetly. "I shall teach her not to be in awe of you. And she and I will sit and laugh at you while you are busy with my errands." Her voice changed to a mixture of eagerness and ill temper. "Renna, there hasn't been any word, has there? No, I was afraid not. That abominable boy." Lady Bradwell's tone was carefully devoid of all but amused exasperation, but Rowena could have cheerfully strangled Lyndon Bradwell on the spot for the look she saw in his mother's eyes. "I know you would inform me immediately had there been— and I still continue to be a plaguey old woman."

"Absolutely impossible," Rowena agreed solemnly.

"But you're paid to put up with my whims, you poor child. Well, perhaps your cousin and I can amuse each other, and if Lyndon does not arrive in time for the party we shall simply enjoy it ourselves. Perhaps I will even proclaim your cousin—what was her name?—to be the guest of honor."

"She would probably be so honored she would blush herself into extinction."

"Likely enough," Lady Bradwell agreed, and settled the hated spectacles on her nose, leaning back into her pillows and searching for her knitting. "Well, if you won't take my wretched John, perhaps your cousin will. A good woman would be his making, but I don't think I could saddle you with John in good conscience."

"Nor saddle Lord Bradwell with me, ma'am. But I warn you that just now Margaret don't seem too keen on the idea of marriage; nothing is so daunting to the spirit as to be badgered to wed."

"If we were to propose the proper party to her, I imagine her delicacy would disappear very quickly. It generally does," Lady Bradwell observed to her knitting.

"It might at that. In which case I can only suppose that no one has ever proposed the proper party to me."

"No, only toadish baronets like that Slyppe fellow, and foolish barons like John." Lady Bradwell sighed. "Well, go along, child, and don't worry about me. I shall be a paragon of invalid virtue. Word of a Bradwell, I shall not read, I shall not stir; I shall sit here and very likely bore myself to death over this shabby genteel knitting."

"You are a wonderful woman," Rowena assured her dryly. "I shall be up again in a little while."

Miss Cherwood departed to give her cousin the good news, then returned to her desk in the office to face again the cards of acceptance, the lists from Cook, the bills from various merchants in the village, and the baffling intricacies of who to seat with whom at dinner.

At the evening meal Lady Bradwell and her eldest son John, Lord Bradwell, were introduced to Miss Margaret Cherwood and expressed much delight in the acquaintance. Margaret, having a hazy romantic notion that as the cousin of Lady Bradwell's companion she should strive to appear as humble as possible, carried only a gauze shawl over her peach-colored evening dress, and shivered quietly in the chill of the dining room until Rowena arrived to send a maid after something more substantial. Lady Bradwell was charmed with the girl's open, affectionate manner and her obvious respect and admiration for her older cousin. Lord Bradwell, on his part, swore that the two young ladies were first-raters, that he could see no difference between Miss Cherwood, in pomona-green crepe, and Miss Margaret in her peach gauze.

"Devilish hard put to say which one of you ladies is the handsomest," he protested, this fulsome compliment rolling awkwardly enough from his usually inarticulate lips to convince all of his sincerity.

"The choice is obvious, my lord." Rowena returned easily. "Your mamma, as always, outshines all of us."

Lady Bradwell, demure and fragile in blue and gray, her hair hidden beneath a charmingly frivolous lace cap, stared down her nose with dignity at her companion, and denounced her for the basest sort of liar.

The company, thus, was in the best of spirits as they sat to dine.

Margaret, whose knowledge of the behavior of ladies and their companions came only from watching her mother's friends, and from the pages of novels, was surprised by the free and easy, unaffected relationship between Lady Bradwell and her cousin. Since Lord Bradwell seemed to find nothing extraordinary in their manner toward each other, Margaret was prepared to accept things as they were. It did occur to her, however, that Lord Bradwell was not, in his own phrase, one of the downy ones, and that while his temper was sweet and his manners gentlemanly, his considered opinions on matters beyond the home farm and the stables were not to be relied upon. Had Lady Bradwell known Miss Margaret's opinion of her elder son she would have given up all thought of a match between the two, but mercifully she was spared it, and continued to amuse herself by plotting quite shamelessly until the tea table arrived.

Shortly after, when they had each had tea and a few biscuits, Miss Cherwood announced that it was far too late for Lady Bradwell to be downstairs. "If you wish to attend the party, ma'am, you must conserve your strength."

"You, miss, are an abominable bully." Lady Bradwell turned to Margaret, protesting, "You see how I am ill used in my own home, child? Well, all right, I suppose I shall never hear the last of it if I do not retire gracefully. Good night, dearest." She offered a cheek to her son to kiss. "Good night, Miss Margaret. I shall enjoy having you here, I think." She smiled again at the girl, then gave her arm to Rowena. "Lead on, tyrant."

"O no, ma'am!" Meg could hear Rowena explaining patiently as she led Lady Bradwell from the room. "You have the cases mixed. *You* are the tyrant and *I* am the tyrannized. I *do* wish you will strive to recall..."

"Wonderful woman, your cousin." Lord Bradwell observed to Margaret. "Keeps Mamma in line with barely a word at it. More than I could ever do, assure you. Game of backgammon?" Margaret mutely assented, and they were finishing the third game when Rowena reappeared to suggest that perhaps they too should retire early. Lord Bradwell said all that was awkward and cordial in his good night, and retired to the library, where he was obviously much more at home. The Misses Cherwood were able to make their way to Rowena's rooms for a comfortable coze.

"But still no sign of the plaguey, prodigal Mr. Bradwell," she mused as they climbed the stairs.

Chapter 2

Rowena had every intention of leaving Margaret with Lady Bradwell the next day, so that she could retire once more to the office and finish with details for the party. She had calculated that one more day's work would do it, which meant that the next day could be spent in frivolities such as mending a dress, writing letters to a number of long-neglected friends, and considering what to wear in the evening for the party. But Lady Bradwell, although she took no exception either to Margaret's company or the general whole of Miss Cherwood's schedule for the day, ordered her companion to spend some part of the afternoon out of doors.

"You look dreadful," she said flatly. "Everyone in the county will say that I have worked you to the bone—certainly I have, but not with an eye to making you lose your looks. This afternoon, *all* afternoon, I want you to ride, or sketch, or walk. Do something in the sun, my dear, and get some of the color back in your face."

"I had no idea I was that pasty-faced, ma'am," Rowena answered, rapidly figuring in her mind what she could displace in order to comply with her mistress's orders and complete her own work. "Well, I shall certainly try to get some time out of doors. But will you—"

"Never mind about me. I shall abuse your cousin's good nature and keep her by me all day—you won't mind too dreadfully, will you, child?—and you may rest assured that she will not let me transgress even one of the doctor's odious rules."

"Well, in that case..." Rowena had visions of the time between three and six, the hour when the dressing bell was rung, spent in sketching the prospect of Broak Hall from the north, at the site of the Diana temple and the rill beside it.

In actuality, it was closer to four than three when Miss Cherwood established herself and her paints by the little brook. "And a wonder I am here before midnight!" she thought, amused. The morning had included a visit by Mr. Greavesey, Dr. Cribbatt's obsequious assistant, as well as a tantrum by Cook, who was in a *mood* again but seemed incapable of explaining exactly what had so upset her. Still, aside from these minor alarums her work had progressed more smoothly than she had expected, and she was able to see the end of her arrangements and list-making in sight.

"Now, if only the prodigal were to decide to stay away!" she hummed under her breath. "I suppose I ought not to be so ready to dislike that man, but his inconsideration surpasses everything, and if his absence throws my lady into a relapse I shall murder him with—with a paintbrush to the heart, if need be!" She added a stroke of green with a vengeful swipe at the paper. It was not so much the extra work that Miss Cherwood objected to: She had been for a long time so used to running her parents' establishments on the continent that the running of a Devonshire country seat was a relatively small matter to her. "Only because I have become an incurable manager," she admitted readily. But Lyndon Bradwell's behavior endangered his mother's peace of mind, and thus her health. After the patient nursing that Miss Cherwood and Taylor, Lady Bradwell's maid, had done over the past six months, Rowena was not prepared to brook any setback.

"Not that Lady B has asked me to shield her from her son!" she admitted. But years of trailing in the wake of her adventurous and travel-mad parents, included as an adult member of their haphazard entourage, attending fetes and tending to the management of their household, had given her a protective attitude toward those she loved which Rowena found difficult to shed. In fourteen years the Cherwoods had lived in India, in the American states, and practically all over Europe (subject, of course, to which countries were under the thumb of the Corsican Monster at any time). Her acquaintance included officers of the staff in Brussels, nabobs in China, and a highly ornamental Marquis in Spain, and Rowena's education had been as original as her upbringing. This idyllic, if original, existence had continued until Waterloo year, when Mr. Cherwood had taken the typhus while helping the wounded that poured into Brussels after the great battle, and had died. Stunned, Rowena and her mother had returned to London, where Mrs. Cherwood, declining gently for almost a year, had followed her husband at last. And Miss Cherwood, left without her beloved and impractical parent to manage for, had gone to the house of her father's brother, Margaret's father. Despite all her best attempts, Rowena was forced to admit at the end of a year that she and her aunt were utterly inimical, and she had begun, over Dorothea Cherwood's outraged protests, to look for employment.

And now: What are we to do with Meggy? she thought absently, washing the page in pale pink. The best, of course, would be to marry her off so that she needn't return home at all, but I doubt that Lord Bradwell is up to her weight.

Who else is there in the neighborhood? Perhaps she could marry the prodigal! The idea made Rowena snort in a very unladylike manner. But not if he's as chuckleheaded as his brother. Or as inconsiderate as he seems to be. What a wretched man. So the subject came full circle back to the irritating Lyndon Bradwell.

"Damnation," she said aloud. Then looked about her from habit, to see if anyone had overheard her unbecoming comment. A blotch of green had dripped from her suspended brush onto the sketch, precisely on the north wall of Broak, over which she had labored for some time. With a soft rag she set about repairing the damage, which work absorbed all her attention for some minutes and thus kept her from ruminating on the shortcomings of Mr. Bradwell. She was not aware of the man strolling toward the house until he was almost beside her.

"Good afternoon," he said, in tones of mild curiosity.

Miss Cherwood jumped, spoiling her picture irredeemably with a startled brush stroke. "Da—do you always creep up on people in that fashion, sir?" she demanded a little breathlessly.

"I hardly crept up on you, Miss—" He paused, but she was too irritated to oblige by supplying her name. "I thought I made rather a great deal of racket, stalking up on the house this way. You *were* rather deep in your work, you know." He gestured toward the ruined paper. "Quite a

ce sketch, except for that streak of brown
cross it—you have captured the color of the
ght at that corner exactly."

"The streak," Rowena informed him icily,
was not intentional. But it's of no import now."

"Was that my fault? Truly, I am sorry." He
spoke with lazy sincerity. Rowena, glaring up
at him, felt her gaze drop again. The stranger
was tall—tall enough so that even had she been
standing, Miss Cherwood would have been
forced to tilt her head up to observe his face. He
was nicely, if not exquisitely, dressed in a coat
of blue superfine, buff pantaloons, and well-pol-
ished Hessian boots, and his light hair was
tossed by the wind—or brushed to give that
effect. His eyes, which she thought were blue
or gray, were his most remarkable feature, dis-
playing intelligence, humor, and kindliness. It
was the kindliness which both won Rowena and
infuriated her. Who *was* this man?

"Do you belong to the house?" he drawled.

"Do I belong there? I'm not chattel goods, sir,
if that's what you mean."

"Good God, no. I assumed that you were a
visitor here, or else a neighbor come to take
advantage of the prospect for sketching. I was
only hoping to ask who I might find at the
house."

"Are you a friend of the Bradwells, sir?" Miss
Cherwood asked. "We are unaccustomed to
seeing pedestrians appear on the grounds at
half-past four, particularly since Lady Bradwell
has been ill." She was emphatic.

28

There was no reaction from the stranger at all. After a moment Rowena decided it was simplest to answer the man's questions. "Lady Bradwell is in, of course, although if you mean to call on her, I wish you will be guided by me and leave her to rest this afternoon: She is in the midst of planning a party for one of her sons, and has been taxing herself more than I can like. She has only been persuaded to rest this afternoon by a combination of efforts. Lord Bradwell I think you might find somewhere about the grounds, but I suspect that he is off with the gamekeeper discussing stock for the pond, or some such."

"Lady Bradwell's giving a party, is she?" The stranger frowned. "What, is Jack getting buckled or something of that sort?"

"No, the party is being held for her other son, who—"

"Damnation!" The stranger snorted. "Why the devil is she taxing herself—I collect that you have not encouraged her in this foolishness. Thank God Mamma is at least surrounded by *some* people of sense. Well, Miss—" He paused, and a look of comprehension came into his eyes, to match the look which had lately come into Rowena's. "You must be Mamma's Dragon! You will forgive me calling you so, but I have been thinking of you that way since I got Mamma's last letter, for you seem to keep her in line, and I know what that must take." He smiled and offered his hand. "I *am* pleased to meet you. I'm Lyn Bradwell."

29

Miss Cherwood, who had reached that conclusion sometime in the middle of this last speech, regarded the hand stretched out to her with mixed feelings, but took it all the same and favored the Prodigal with a very halfhearted smile of welcome. That his coming had overset his mother was bad enough, but that he should introduce himself to her in a fashion guaranteed to put her at a disadvantage (as well as having made her spoil a very promising watercolor) was really too bad.

"I am sorry," he added after a moment's uncomfortable silence. "But I regret to admit that I cannot recall your name. I had grown so used to thinking of you as—"

"The Dragon," Rowena supplied sweetly. "Well, if you tire of that form of address, Mr. Bradwell, you may call me Miss Cherwood," she finished coolly.

"Now you're at outs with me." Bradwell sighed. Rowena had begun to rinse out her brushes and fold her painting kit away. "But you must realize that I had been envisioning a much older woman, sort of a—"

"Dragon," Miss Cherwood repeated succinctly, although her sense of the ridiculous was slowly reasserting itself and her tone was less venomous than it had been a moment before. "It's quite all right, Mr. Bradwell. I regret, of course, that I cannot oblige you by being the martinet of forty you expected, but I assure you that I am older than I may appear, and quite capable of keeping your mother from overtaxing her strength under most ordinary circumstances. But she would have this party, thirty couples from the neighborhood, indeed, and everything fine about it—"

"Except that you don't think Mamma's health is up to it."

"It may be, sir, if she will let me have the ordering of things and will refrain from wasting strength on unnecessaries," she admitted, folding up the little stool on which she had been sitting. Bradwell reached to take it from her, but she had already placed it atop her painting box and was setting off in the direction of the house. Mr. Bradwell was beginning to form the impression that, despite her pretty face and slender figure, Miss Cherwood was indeed a dragon of sorts.

"I had no idea Mamma would do anything so idiotish—" he began.

"It's hardly idiotish to wish to welcome home her prodigal son, gone these six years," Rowena began hotly, in defense of her mistress.

"Five," Bradwell corrected mildly. "And I'm not criticizing the thought, Miss Dragon-Cherwood, but that fact that Mamma was silly enough to think I would expect a party of her when she is so lately out of the sickroom." There was nothing in that speech that Rowena could take exception to; in fact, it was a reiteration of many of her thoughts on the subject. She found herself a little more in charity with Bradwell, although she could not remember the last time she had been so in and out of favor toward anyone in such a short time.

"Can you tell me how Mamma is going on aside from taking too much upon herself with this party, as we have both agreed?"

"The doctor says she has mended remarkably, and that it is only her eyes we must take especial care of. She hates to wear her spectacles—blue glass, and not tremendously becoming—and will do so only with the greatest reluctance. And when I have tried to interest her in things that will not strain her eyes she throws up the most imaginative obstacles! I taught her to knit, and she is perfectly adept to it, only says it is shabby genteel and won't be seen by anyone but me while she does it. You may see that her temper is improved. Or worsened, rather, but I think it is a good sign."

"But her eyes? What is the danger there?"

"It is hard for me to say, exactly, when even Dr. Cribbatt dislikes to test them too far for fear of straining them. Lady Bradwell goes without the spectacles in the house, and can see quite clearly now, although she is still forbidden close work and reading and writing. And on no account must she go into the daylight without those spectacles, no matter what she says."

"And I wager she's the very devil to persuade about them, ain't she?" Bradwell smiled. "She's a vain puss, is Mamma. Should I tease her about them?"

"Sir, if you've half the influence with her that I imagine you have, I think she will wrap herself in blue glass if she thinks you would like it," Miss Cherwood advised drily.

"Coming it a bit too strong, Miss Cherwood. I apologized for ruining your painting, didn't I? What other crimes—other than calling you a dragon, but I will be excused for that, won't I, since my image of you was so far from the reality—of what else am I accused?" He smiled again at her; it was really a very nice smile, and lit his fine eyes. They were gray, Rowena decided. "You think me abominably rag-mannered, don't you? My only excuse is that I am only just returned from seeking my fortune on the continent, and I have forgotten the common civilities of an English drawing room."

"And did you find your fortune, Mr. Bradwell?" Miss Cherwood asked sweetly.

"I'm afraid that the people who arrived before me had completely cleared the palaces of the continent of their treasures, Miss Cherwood. I have hopes of making my way in the Foreign Office, but I will have to acquire some more contacts than the ones I made through my soldiering days."

Rowena sighed. "I suppose if you had tried the drawing rooms on the continent you would have discovered more useful contacts there. *I* never had the least difficulty in recalling what was due the English drawing room, for I found the drawing rooms of France and Spain and Portugal and Austria to be very similar to the ones in Devon and Sussex."

"I suspect that was a setdown, Miss Cherwood. Have you actually lived in any of those places?"

"All of them, Mr. Bradwell. But I promise not to contradict you in front of your Mamma." Rowena gave him a smile and entered the house.

"I must say, Mamma," Mr. Bradwell commented later, when the first flush of their reunion was over, "that that Miss Cherwood of yours—"

"Rowena? Isn't she the greatest love in creation, Lyn? I cannot tell you how good and how patient she has been with me, aside from taking over all the management of the house while I was so ill, although that was by no means expected of her."

Lyndon Bradwell, still unsettled by his meeting with his mother's companion, thought that perhaps seizing the management of the household would be the more precise term, but wisely refrained from voicing it.

"Jack, even, thinks that she is a good creature, and you know that the last female of whom Jack said any such thing—always aside from his mares, of course—was Jane Ambercot. Of course, Rowena is too wise to think they would do anything but bore each other to death if he offered for her. Although I could almost wish, for Jack's sake, that she would take him."

Mr. Bradwell disregarded the disquieting idea of Miss Rowena Cherwood as his sister-in-law. "No, I don't think a strong-minded female past her first youth is quite the thing for Jack, Mamma."

"What a fashion in which to describe Rowena, you monster. Lyn, you haven't taken her in dislike, have you? I only meant that if Jack will not reconsider Jane—and yes, I know better than to try to raise that engagement again, even though everyone knew they would have been terribly happy together—where was I?—O yes, well, sometimes I wish that Jack had not been such a fool."

"I see very little comparison between Miss Ambercot and Miss Cherwood, Mamma."

"Well, in looks, certainly not. Jane, fond of her as I am, *does* have the most annoying tendency to freckle, and she is rather short, and the only dress that really suits her is riding habit. But she and Jack would have suited so well together, I can't mind her appearance at all. I do regret their quarrel sometimes."

"So does Jack, I'm sure," Mr. Bradwell observed thoughtfully. "There's also rather a disparity between your Miss Cherwood and Miss Ambercot, as I recall, in temper."

"They're both commonsensical creatures, Lyn, and I know that Jane would have managed Jack to a nicety."

"Just as your Miss Cherwood sees to you, ma'am?" He wondered privately if this Miss Cherwood was not something of an opportunist.

"Precisely. But Lyn, you've been sitting here in my room for above an hour, and have not told me how long you intend to stay."

"In your room, Mamma?" He raised a quizzing eyebrow.

"Stupid, idiotish creature. At Broak. In England. Within an easy distance of your poor, abandoned mother!"

"O, as for that, I am back for good. In England, at least."

"Truly? Lyn, I'm so pleased! But what do you mean to do?"

"Do, Mamma?" he teased.

"Don't play games with me, boy. I know, if you do not, that you no more have the character to sit about and waste your time than your father did. But Richard had the estate to occupy him, and Jack has that now, so what do you mean to do?"

"Well, to tell the truth, Uncle Kelvin and I had a notion that a job in the government might suit me—"

"Politics, darling?" Lady Bradwell frowned. "But my dear, doesn't that take a great deal of money? Or many connections."

"It can take both, Mamma, and while I have a small amount of money and two or three connections—beyond my uncle, of course—I realize that I shall have to set myself up to find myself a niche and bide my time in gathering both the ready and the connections to advance in the party. Uncle Kelvin has given me some letters to submit to his friends in London, and I do have an advantage in that I have been abroad in A'Court's retinue and have a good idea of what diplomacy on the continent has become since '15."

"Well, if it is what you want to do. All I can think of when you say politics is poor Georgiana Devonshire selling her kisses for Fox's sake in the elections."

"That was rather a while ago, ma'am, and I doubt that I shall ever attach a woman who will dispense kisses to the hoi polloi a-purpose to see me elected. In any case—" He rose. "I believe there is someone at the door."

It was Rowena Cherwood. "Good evening, ma'am." She smiled at her mistress with such obvious affection that Mr. Bradwell questioned his own assumptions regarding his mother's companion. "I was wondering if I ought to tell Cook to set dinner back half an hour."

"Was that the dressing bell?" Lady Bradwell asked in surprise.

"It was."

"Then you must send Taylor in to help me dress. Lyn, I shall see you at dinner. If Miss Margaret Cherwood is downstairs, I wish you will introduce yourself to her. She's the least bit shy, but she's a very sweet little thing."

"*Margaret* Cherwood?" Mr. Bradwell's glance returned to Rowena with suspicion.

"My cousin," she announced defiantly. "She came asking my help—some family matters, but your mamma was kind enough to offer her asylum."

"A very romantical story, Lyn. If you see her, please entertain her until we can join you. She

37

looks very much like Rowena, as a matter of fact."

"Well, she looks much as I did when I was her age," Miss Cherwood conceded. "Now, ma'am, do you intend to dress for dinner or no?"

"See, I am bullied shamelessly in my own house," Lady Bradwell protested laughingly to her son. "Go along, darling. I shall see you below directly."

Lyndon Bradwell left the room, another point against Miss Cherwood firmly entered in his books. Invite a strange cousin here to trespass on his mother's hospitality? Even if the girl herself were unexceptionable, it bespoke something of Miss Rowena's attitude toward her position at Broak. Mr. Bradwell did not like it.

But when he made Margaret Cherwood's acquaintance that evening (and she did look remarkably like her cousin, only younger, sweeter, and with an endearing shyness which he was certain Miss Rowena had never possessed) he was ready to rearrange his ideas once again. By the time Lady Bradwell, Lord Bradwell, and Miss Cherwood joined them in the small saloon, Mr. Bradwell and Miss Margaret considered themselves fast friends. Lady Bradwell, looking from Lyn to Margaret to Lyn, and then to Rowena, invited her secretly to share in her matchmaking plot. Rowena returned the smile rather inscrutably, and comforted herself with the thought that at least Lady Bradwell, Margaret, and Lyndon Bradwell could be safely left to entertain each other while she attended to the business of Broak, and to the party. Lord Brad-well, of course, could be depended to settle himself with the grooms and keep from underfoot.

So, she thought, the Prodigal was home at last; the guest of honor would bless the company with his presence at the party, and all, finally, must be right with the world.

Chapter 3

Thankfully, at least in Miss Cherwood's opinion, she was kept much too busy with the superintendence of minutiae, and Mr. Bradwell was much too occupied in entertaining his mother and Margaret with stories of Madrid and with reacquainting himself with his home, for them to meet much. When she thought of Lady Bradwell's prodigal son at all, it was either to wonder how such a sweet-tempered parent could have raised such an objectionable son, or to reflect with thanks on how well Lyndon Bradwell, Lady Bradwell, and Margaret seemed to be going along. Having left Margaret with strict instructions that Lady Bradwell was on no account to overtax her strength or to strain her eyes, Rowena was able to turn her attention to the last pressing issues of silver, champagne, and iced cup.

Now and again Margaret, or Mr. Bradwell, or even, on one memorable occasion, Lord Bradwell, turned up at the office door inquiring if there were errands to be run. Margaret she dismissed with the admonition that the best thing *she* could do was to keep Lady Bradwell company; to Lyn Bradwell she said she would not hear of the guest of honor running errands for his own party; and when Lord Bradwell offered his assistance, Rowena went so far as to tell Lyn that the kindest effort he could make would be to keep his lordship out of the house and away from the office. Mr. Bradwell, after a moment's surprise, agreed blandly, and a few minutes later Rowena heard him unenthusiastically requesting his brother's company for an hour's ride.

Left alone with the last of her lists and the occasional company of Drummey, Mrs. Coffee, and the chief groom, Rowena was pleased to organize the final details of Lady Bradwell's party into complete readiness.

Mounting the stairs to her room that evening to dress for the party, Rowena at last allowed herself some of the old, breathless anticipation before a party, amusing herself with outlandish images of hairstyles and ribbons. In her room she found her best evening dress, a silk muslin in lavender, lavishly sprigged in white, with worked flounces, a fichu of netted silk, and rows of tiny crystal beads at the low neck and sleeves. Frowning, Rowena rang for her maid.

"Ruth, I asked that the green muslin be laid out," she began severely.

"So you did say, miss," the girl agreed broadly. "But her lady said you was to wear the best you had, miss; called me special into her room to tell me so, and never you mind about that Miss Margaret, for her lady's found her something ever so pretty," the maid finished apologetically.

"Machinations behind my back! Well, I shall have to scold her for it, shan't I?" Rowena said lightly. "Thank you, Ruth."

Hot water was poured from the tin can into the basin; the fire was stirred up, and still the maid stood there, awkwardly. "Yes?" Rowena asked at last, wondering what was coming now.

"O, miss, do you think I could stay and help you dress? It ain't just for me, like; I know I'm a clumsy sort, but I've three little sisters, and if I could tell 'em, on my next half-day—"

"That you helped me prepare for the ball?" Rowena asked with amusement. "Very well, you may stay if you like." So when Miss Cherwood had done washing, and had skillfully applied a touch of Pomade of Roses to her cheeks, a light scattering of rice powder on her face, Ruth helped her to don the lavender gown, and brushed out her long, chestnut-brown hair. At last Rowena repossessed herself of the brush, and in a few quick motions twisted the bulk of her hair into an intricate pile atop her head, fastened in two amethyst combs, threw a light scarf across her shoulders, and declared that she was ready. Ruth, conscious of the honor done her, was lavish in her praise of Miss Cherwood's appearance. Rowena laughed, thanked her, and dispatched her back to the servants' hall. After one more cursory glance in the mirror she left the room to join the party in the dining room.

Dinner was planned as a simple meal that evening, since supper would be served a few hours hence. Lady Bradwell, waiting with her sons and Margaret in the library (and Lady Bradwell had indeed found a charming gown for Margaret, although Rowena could not imagine how it had been done on such short notice), complimented both the Misses Cherwood on their appearance, and all went in to dinner in high spirits, to be entertained for the entire of the meal by one of Lord Bradwell's interminable hunting stories.

Having organized the household for the party, Rowena now deferred to Lady Bradwell, who looked to be enjoying the office of hostess immensely. She and her sons stood at receiving for a short while, but the list of guests was not long enough to make that an arduous task, and the spirit of the evening was informal enough to allow them to cut the duty shorter still. On the arrival of her dear friend and long-absent neighbor Anne Ambercot, Lady Bradwell was content to sit and coze comfortably by the fire, adjured strictly to wear her spectacles no matter how irksome she might find them. Lyn Bradwell went in search of Margaret Cherwood and Lord Bradwell made his way to the library, where masculine noise proclaimed that the brandy was circulating.

Margaret was to be found with her cousin, and was in fact delivering a stern lecture. The effect of little Margaret scolding her tall cousin was much the same as a spaniel hectoring a mastiff, and Mr. Bradwell had to school himself to greet them both with equanimity.

"Rowena, I wish you will not be so goose-ish," Miss Margaret was saying as he drew nearer. "You know that Lady Bradwell has *told* you that you were to enjoy yourself this evening; you have worked hard enough, after all. Now will you cease to act like such a—a—" She faltered.

"A companion, Meggy? It is, after all, what I am. I have a certain responsibility to Lady Bradwell, after all, and forgetting her is exactly what I ought not to do. Besides which, I really am beyond the age and the inclination to get myself up a flirtation."

Margaret blushed. "I never suggested that, Renna! But Lady Bradwell strictly enjoined you—"

She was interrupted by Lyndon Bradwell. "I think Miss Margaret has the right of it, Miss Cherwood. This is not a formal party, after all, and we are not the sort of toplofty gudgeons to deny you your evening's jollification. You told

45

me yesterday that I was the guest of honor at this fete. In that case I wish you will please me and join the throng like a sensible creature." The words were spoken to Rowena, but it was at Margaret that he looked, and to Margaret that he offered his arm.

"In that case, sir,"—Rowena smiled drily— "I can hardly refuse. I shall follow you in and make myself—Good heavens, Lully Ambercot!"

Margaret and Mr. Bradwell regarded her with some amazement. They were joined a moment later by a gentleman who seemed quite as flabbergasted as Miss Cherwood.

"Renna Cherwood?" he asked in tones of disbelief. "It is! Does Mamma know you are here? And Jane and Lizzie? Good God, how long has it been?" He gave every indication of intending to give Rowena a most brotherly sort of bear hug, but she put out a hand and told him sternly that if he crushed her dress she would never forgive him.

"But do you know Mr. Bradwell?" she continued. The two gentlemen nodded cursorily. "And this is my cousin Margaret Cherwood. Ulysses Ambercot, Meggy."

Margaret smiled. In fact, Margaret veritably sparkled at the tall, fair stranger with the brush of pale hair and strong, bony features. "How do you do, sir?"

Mr. Ambercot relinquished his hold on Rowena for a moment to take Margaret's hand. "Better every minute, Miss Margaret, believe me." And then, returning to Rowena, "But you must tell me where in thunderation you have been these—Lord knows how many years. And first I must take you to see Mamma. You see her there, by the fire with Lady Bradwell." And before Miss Cherwood could make more than a dip to Mr. Bradwell and her cousin, Mr. Ambercot had taken her hand in his arm and led her away.

"How do you come to know the Bradwells, Renna? You and that pretty cousin of yours?"

"I'm here as companion to Lady Bradwell, Lully."

He stopped in his tracks. "A companion? You? Leaving aside the fact that I *know* you must be rolling in the blunt, Renna, I can't imagine you cooped up when you could be having adventures like the old times."

"Could I? My dear, the greatest amount of money in the world could not excuse the impropriety of my doing on my own as I was used to do with Mamma and Papa. Even if I engaged a veritable battalion of companion-chaperones I couldn't travel as we used to do, and I should probably be bored to tears regardless of the adventures I had with a flock of old ladies chivying me."

"Well, then, why ain't you married with a parcel of brats? I thought I heard something about that several years back, when you were in Brussels, just before—" he paused.

"Just before Papa died? Why, yes, I was engaged to a very fine young lieutenant in the first Heavy Dragoons—the Royals. Fortunately, we agreed we should not suit, and jilted each other. That was just before Waterloo, and what might have been a nine-day wonder was swallowed up in all the confusion soon after."

"And no one since? Rowena, you were on your way to becoming a real Diamond when I last saw you, and the bucks of St. James's could hardly have ignored you—"

"Nor did they, when Mamma and I returned to London. But we were in mourning then, and in any case, what makes you think I wanted a buck of St. James's? I simply never met anyone I wished to marry. I was abroad—where were we? Paris, I think, when I should have made my come-out and gone to Almack's and all the rest, and somehow I never *did*. After Mamma died I lived with my Aunt Dorothea—Margaret's mother—for a time, but what I saw in her household did not convince me of the virtues of the convenient marriage! And now, can you imagine how I would show to advantage among all the chits six or seven years younger than I at the assemblies? Margaret takes the wind all out of my sails, you know."

"Nonsense," he chaffed. "And how came you here?"

"I asked my man of business to find a situation for me, somewhere where I would be needed. It did seem, after all, somewhat better than playing ape-leader from my aunt's house. But enough of that. Tell me, how is Auntie Anne?"

"If I am not mistaken," Ambercot said wryly,

"she and Lady Bradwell are busy making matches for all of us, and are quite happy at it, too. And see, there is Jane talking with Angelica Hardimann, and Eliza—O lord, Rowena, let me warn you about Eliza."

"Warn me about her? Why, is she dangerous?"

"Not exactly. Just a plaguey nuisance. Since my aunt Berring took her to Bath for two months the chit's been the most irritating piece of nature imaginable. Calls herself Lisette, or at very least Eliiii-zah, and thinks she can outshine a regular stunner at ten paces. And has assumed all the airs to go with it. Mamma thinks she's amusing, and so too would I, I suppose, if I hadn't the horrid notion that she shan't outgrow it. Lizzie was always the most contrary chit."

"Don't brothers always think that of their sisters?" Rowena suggested.

"I don't say anything of the sort about Jane. Lizzie's too spoilt by half, if you ask me. M'father made a pet of her, if you recall. So if Lizzie starts to come the debutante with you, give her a proper setdown, I beg."

"When have you ever known me to give anyone anything so odious as a setdown?" Miss Cherwood quizzed.

"Any number of times. You may have only been a scrawny thing of fourteen when last I saw you, Rowena, but damme if you hadn't the presence of a dowager in purples even then. And I seem to recall a remarkable proficiency in the

profanities of the French and Spanish tongues."
They had begun to move toward Lady Bradwell
and Mrs. Ambercot again, and the latter, suddenly recognizing in Rowena the precocious,
coltish girl she had last seen a dozen years before, broke off her chattering to call her son to
her.

"Rowena Cherwood, is that truly you?"

"I must suppose so, ma'am," Miss Cherwood
replied, bending to kiss the older woman affec-
tionately.

"Rowena, you never told me you knew the
Ambercots!" Lady Bradwell accused.

"I don't believe I ever thought of it, ma'am.
If you recall, you never told *me* that *you* knew
them either."

"I must have mentioned Jane to you, telling
you about Jack."

"I believe you did, but only as that Dear
Jane...with a sigh at the end of it. For a fact,
I've known the Ambercots all my life: My
father's seat in Cambridgeshire marched on
their house there, and I grew up tormenting Mr.
Ambercot and his sisters."

"No, I beg to correct you!" Ulysses Ambercot
insisted. "It was only *me* you tormented. Jane
and Lizzie you seemed to like well enough—"

"Eliza was much too young to play with you
hoyden children then," Mrs. Ambercot interrupted her son's accusations repressively. "But
my dearest child, you look absolutely beautiful!
And very much like your papa."

"Do you think so, ma'am? Aunt Dorothea was

wont to say that I hadn't a trace of Cherwood looks in me, or—"

"Exactly the sort of thing I should have expected from Dorothea Cherwood. A dreadful woman. Ulysses, fetch Jane to me; I'm sure she will want to make her curtsies to Rowena after all these years." Mr. Ambercot acceded gracefully to the command, made his bow, and went in search of his sister. "Renna, my dear, there was a time when your mamma and I had such plans for you and Ulysses, and indeed, if I thought it would make you happy I would join your hands myself and carol 'Bless You My Children' with a will to it."

"But it wouldn't fadge in the least," Lady Bradwell objected firmly.

"Don't you mind her, Auntie Anne. She wants me for Lord Bradwell," Miss Cherwood teased. "But she is right. I like Lully too well to marry him."

"O, I gave up *that* dream some time ago; I think it was when you pushed Lully into the punch bowl at the Christmas party such a long time ago. I surmised in an instant that Lully simply wasn't up to your weight. O drat!"

Lady Bradwell and Miss Cherwood turned in surprise to see what had made Mrs. Ambercot exclaim with such vehemence.

"I do beg your pardon, my dears. It's only that dreadful Eliza of mine. I can't allow Lully to speak ill of her, but for myself, I will allow that this nonsense of hers has almost brought me to my wit's end. Look at her, languishing on Jack's arm! What a dreadful child it is." Indeed, Miss Eliza Ambercot could be seen hanging on the arm of a rather rattled-looking Lord Bradwell.

"Quite unlike Ulysses and Jane," Lady Bradwell agreed, straining to locate Miss Ambercot in the crowd. "Lord, I loathe these abominable things!" she announced, removing her detested spectacles from her nose, despite Rowena's admonitory cluckings. "Where is Jane? I haven't seen her since you arrived."

"I fancy she's talking with one of Squire Polwyn's boys now, about the hunt last year. Consider me, Louisa," Mrs. Ambercot said mournfully to Lady Bradwell. "A fribble for a son, one daughter more at home at the hunt than in the drawing room, and one who is determined that she will marry a Duke—a Royal Duke for preference, an' she can find one not too corpulent."

"Are any of them left unmarried?" Rowena asked with interest, and was rewarded with a comical look of dislike from Lady Bradwell and Mrs. Ambercot.

"I have often wondered, Rowena—" Lady Bradwell began repressively, but broke off as Jane Ambercot joined them. Miss Ambercot was a neat stocky woman with a squarish sort of face, a square, short figure, and square, short-fingered hands; her manner was forthright and rather engaging. Just now her pleasant, freckled countenance was alight with smiles as she offered her hand to Miss Cherwood.

"Good evening, Lady Bradwell. Hullo, Mamma, are you bemoaning your children again?

Rowena?" This last was said with a touch of shyness.

"Hello, Jane," Miss Cherwood returned, and gave her old friend a quick kiss. "How pretty you look."

"O certainly," Miss Ambercot agreed wryly. "Quite like a plow horse dressed in muslin. *You* look pretty. Do you know, Lady Bradwell, that when I was eleven, and Miss Cherwood fourteen, I wanted nothing more in the world than to look just like her—"

"Jane, you must be funning. At fourteen I was a complete bean pole—"

"With masses of beautiful hair, and so tall and slender! And here I am, defeated by my freckles and my resemblance to poor Papa." She made a rueful movement with her hands. "Somehow I always expect to find pockets, and they're never there."

"You're not in riding dress, Jane," Mrs. Ambercot reproved.

Lady Bradwell, charmed with these insights about her companion, nevertheless was bound to do her duty as a hostess. "Children, it is time we sent you back into the party and continued our gossiping."

"Shall we return to find ourselves married off, and everything tidy?" Rowena teased.

"Why, certainly," Lady Bradwell agreed.

"In that case, I shan't stay about to hear my fate." Rowena took Jane's elbow and the two left the older women to their talk.

"Have you met my cousin Margaret?" Rowena asked.

"Renna, I haven't seen you in I don't know how many years. I'd no idea you *had* a Cousin Margaret. Is she here?"

"Yes, I left her talking with Lady Bradwell's prodigal son—damnation, will I never learn to guard my tongue? Pray forget that you heard me say that. Meg arrived a few days ago, chased from her home, if you can believe anything so gothic, by her Mamma, who wanted her to marry a man twice her age."

"Does romance simply run in your family, Renna?" Jane grinned. "At least you always had your Mamma and Papa to play chaperone on your adventures."

"On the contrary, I played *their* chaperone. Mamma could be relied upon to be arguing with Portuguese housekeepers who spoke no English, and Papa might be found trading stories with the soldiers. Any soldiers, at that! He would as readily have spoken with Bonaparte's fellows as with our own. And probably did, too, which is why he was such a famous diplomat." She smiled reminiscently for a moment. "But look, there's my cousin. Margaret, dear"—she hailed Meg, who was obviously in search of her. "Meg, this is Mr. Ambercot's sister Jane, who was my playmate when Mamma and Papa and I lived in Cambridgeshire."

"Miss Cherwood, I hope we shall be friends, for if you ain't my friend, then I suppose my sister will try to make you hers, and I wouldn't wish such a fate on you." Miss Ambercot extended her hand and smiled in a friendly manner. "And there's Lully again. I have the most lowering suspicion—" Jane began.

"Yes?" Rowena prodded.

"Nothing. Impolitic. Do you like Devon, Miss Margaret?" Miss Ambercot asked hastily.

"Of course she does," Ulysses Ambercot answered. "Miss Cherwood"—this was obviously addressed to Margaret—"might I beg your company for a turn around the room? I shall explain, if you wish, exactly what about Devonshire it is that you like."

"Mayn't I form my own opinions, sir?" Margaret asked breathlessly.

"All the better, of course," he agreed solemnly, and led her off.

"I have a suspicion that Lully is going to be smitten by your cousin," Jane said.

"I have very much the same suspicion," Rowena agreed. "Well, you shall talk with her another time, then. Is that you or me your mamma is beckoning to?"

"Me, I fear. Either my flounces are torn or my hair is coming down, or perhaps she just wants me to fetch her some claret cup. Shall I see you later?"

"I hope so." Miss Ambercot began to pick her way through the groups of people, toward the fireplace. Rowena settled herself in a chair nearby, content for a few minutes to watch the product of her hard work: the party's smooth process.

"I collect that you know the Ambercots *very* well," a voice behind her commented drily.

"I beg your pardon?" She turned to face Lyndon Bradwell.

"What was that ridiculous thing you called Mr. Ambercot?"

"Lully? Short for Ulysses, which Eliza could not pronounce as a baby. He and Jane and I were playmates as children. He used," she continued reminiscently, "to tie me up with the sash of my own gown, and I would escape and come after him in some dreadful retribution...."

"What sort of retribution?" Bradwell asked, piqued.

"O very ungentlemanly sorts, I assure you, since I hadn't the strength to thrash him as I would have liked to do. I recall inquiring in a very loud voice in Auntie Anne's drawing room one afternoon whatever Lully had done with the monstrous fine snake he had brought to the house. *That* put the household into some uproar, I can promise you. I should rather have tied him up in turn, you know, but as I had little hope of that, I was forced upon my wits."

"Obviously," Mr. Bradwell agreed equably, much amused by the pictures his mother's companion painted for him. Rowena wondered privately when she had so far recovered from her dislike of the man as to have been able to recount this absurd story, and found herself baffled by the question.

"Can you tell me," she continued rather hurriedly, "if that lady with your brother can possibly be Eliza Ambercot?"

"Frankly I cannot, since the acquaintance between their family and mine dates from about the time I left for Spain. I did meet Miss Jane and her brother at Jack's betrothal party, of course, but Miss Eliza was still in the nursery at the time. I suspect it may be she; she rather resembles your Lully."

"Hardly *mine*. And the last time *I* saw Lizzie Ambercot, she was five years old, throwing a tantrum over a sweetmeat."

"I can well imagine it." He agreed, observing the girl more closely. "Well, if Jack likes to have her hand on him—although I know well that he does not, and cannot sufficiently convey this to her—he is welcome to her. Far better him than I."

"Poor Eliza," Miss Cherwood said, with little sympathy.

"Poor Eliza indeed. I wish you could imbue her with a little of your own reluctance to move about in the company, Miss Cherwood. I haven't a doubt it would become her better."

"Are you bamming me, sir?" Rowena regarded her companion suspiciously.

"Not in the least, ma'am. Why should you think so?"

"When you make a silly statement such as that, for all the world as if I were entirely given over to old lace, dowager's cap, and lavender ribbons! Just because I am sensible of my responsibilities...."

"Highly sensible," he said, with the curl to his lips that had so infuriated her when they met. Rowena rose as if to leave. "No, ma'am, I am sorry. Don't let me drive you from your seat. I was only referring to the words which I heard you speak to Miss Margaret earlier. I assure you, my mother considers you with as much—more, in fact—pleasure and friendliness than she does my sisters."

"I beg your pardon if I seem too sensitive, Mr. Bradwell, but you see, I am still a little unused to this business of being in a *position,* and sometimes I do not know just what to make of it."

"Don't fret yourself with it too much, Miss Cherwood. Consider yourself one of our family, as Mamma and Jack already do."

"And you?"

"When I know you better, I assume I shall do as well," he said easily. It was not a very satisfying answer. "Damnation. Jack's cast Eliza Ambercot off at last and she's directed herself here. I hate to be uncivil, Miss Cherwood, but I think I find myself in need of a stiff brandy. At once."

"Certainly, Mr. Bradwell. I'll make your apologies," Rowena countered. He shot her a puzzled look, then smiled and took his leave. Miss Cherwood, left alone again, smoothed her skirt and prepared herself for the onslaught of Miss Eliza Ambercot and her dainty manner.

Chapter 4

Regrettably, Eliza Ambercot fully justified her brother's unkindly aspersions. After claiming Miss Cherwood as a cherished acquaintance, with many ill-pronounced phrases in French to back this claim, she proceeded to give Rowena a complete *histoire* of the family since their last meeting. As the tale was mostly comprised of a listing of every beau with whom Eliza had danced at the Bath assemblies, with animadversions upon "Poor Jane's misfortunate engagement," and "Lully's shocking luck at cards," it is not wonderful that Miss Cherwood shortly was overwhelmed with a desire to escape. Eliza was finishing her monologue with a flowery prayer that Miss Cherwood would be as desirous as she of regaining their former intimacy when she espied Lyndon Bradwell across the room and rather hurriedly took her leave. As this saved Rowena from making the admission that the only intimacy *she* could recall was when she had helped Ulysses to lock Eliza in the milking shed one afternoon, she was more than happy to let the girl go.

Ulysses, deprived of Margaret's smiles for a moment, returned to Rowena's side, murmuring an adjuration that she wasn't to take anything his sister said too seriously.

"Good God, Lully, but how could I? O, that poor little thing, has she *no* idea of what a guy she makes of herself?"

"None," Mr. Ambercot assured her.

"And I ought not to say such things to you, I collect."

"Nonsense, Renna, when you've known Lizzie since she was in leading strings! And I'm the first to admit that the chit's an aggravation to man and child alike. What all did she tell you?"

"It was mostly a compendium of Captain Shaw and Mr. Treaton and Lieutenant Beale, and the gowns she wore to the Bath assemblies. O dear, I see"— Rowena bit her tongue, but Ulysses had caught her drift immediately.

"Cornered Bradwell, hasn't she. Well, he put up a gallant fight, I'll say that for him. And she's talked the ears off everyone else at the party, I don't see why he oughtn't to do his job."

A little uncomfortable in this line of conversation, Rowena stumbled upon another topic, equally unacceptable but of far greater interest to her: "What is this Eliza told me of Jane's engagement?"

Mr. Ambercot had the grace to assume a more sober mien. "It was awkward enough, I can tell you. Jane was engaged to Jack Bradwell three years ago; I should have thought they'd suit each other down to the ground, too, but not three weeks before the ceremony, Jane cried off. Seems Jack was flirting with some female or other at one of Mamma's parties in Town— rather a *warm* little thing, too; Mamma should have known better!—and Jane reproached him for it, and *he* told her not to be such a fool, and— well, there it was. Mamma was sending in a 'regretfully announce' to the *Gazette*. *I* am of the opinion," he added pontifically, "that they are both about in their heads, and will never find anyone they can like as well as each other."

"I never fail to be amazed at the ways in which people contrive to be miserable," Rowena agreed wryly. She might, indeed, have continued, but Ulysses noticed that Margaret was talking with his mother now, and felt a sudden filial urge overpower him. Rowena graciously accepted his awkward apology and watched him thread through the crowd toward her cousin. She wondered, as she watched, whether Margaret might not solve her own problem by marrying Lully—if not so old or mean-tempered a suitor as the unlamented Lord Slyppe, Mr. Ambercot was very nearly as wealthy, which was certain to assure his eligibility in the eyes of Margaret's mother.

It was not much longer until Lady Bradwell reluctantly agreed that she *was* fatigued, and permitted Rowena to help her to her room and ring for her maid. Although the party continued for some time after the departure of the hostess, by the time Rowena reappeared in the hall, Lord Bradwell and his brother were sending the last of the guests out to their carriages. Feeling that domestic matters could safely be left to the staff, Rowena collected her shawl and a rather sleepy Margaret from the drawing room, and retired for the night.

In the morning Miss Cherwood thought to be the only person so early at breakfast, perhaps the only one at all. She had seen both Lord Bradwell and his brother retire to the library to fortify themselves with brandy, and suspected that they had returned there when the last guest was gone, to drink rather deeply to the evening's success. She was surprised, therefore, to find Lyn Bradwell seated in the breakfast room, desultorily picking at a plate of eggs and bacon, and reading the London papers. He looked up when she entered, smiled and rose from his seat, folding the paper.

"There's no need to do that on my account," she said as she inspected the array of chafing dishes on the sideboard.

"Surely you cannot like to eat your breakfast

confronted by the back pages of the *Times?*" Bradwell protested.

"I assure you, I am quite used to do so. My father was not a fit conversationalist if deprived of his morning paper, and my mother was not a fit conversationalist if awakened at any time before noon. I early became adept at amusing myself between the kippers and the jam."

"I admire you for it, but I had almost done with the papers anyway. How do you do this morning?"

Helping herself to beef, egg, and a few waferish slices of toast, Rowena settled herself and poured her tea. "May I offer you some hot? I am very well, and pleased to see the house in such good order after last evening."

"You've been inspecting already?" Bradwell raised a quizzing eyebrow.

"Certainly. It only takes a minute or so to look through the public rooms, and to ask Mrs. Coffee how everything went on. And to tell truth, I am surprised to see anyone else about this morning."

"You take my family for very shabby stock, Miss Cherwood."

"Not in the least, but you will at least admit that I was not very far wrong, was I? I know Meggy was quite done up when I left her in her room, between the party itself and the excitements of the last few days. And that your mamma should spend the next few days abed to recover herself is certainly not odd. But you know my views on *that* subject."

"If you mean her folly in giving the party at all, I imagine our ideas march very closely. You blame me for it, I collect?"

"Not at all, sir, unless you wrote your mamma a letter I did not read to her which commanded that—"

"That the fatted calf be slaughtered, Miss Cherwood? The image is yours, you know."

"I apologize for a stupid remark, Mr. Bradwell, and would consider it highly obliging in you if you would forget I ever made it. To continue my first line of thought: To be quite frank, I suspected, after seeing you and Lord Bradwell retire to the library last night, that neither of you would wish to arise early this morning. Certainly not if you had been making depredations of a heavy sort."

"Very mild depredations, Miss Cherwood. Mine, at least. I collect that Jack was a trifle rattled to see Jane Ambercot—not to mention having that beastly little schoolroom chit hanging on his elbow half the night."

"Entirely dreadful, ain't she," Miss Cherwood agreed sympathetically, recalling that Lord Bradwell's was not the only elbow to which Miss Eliza had attached herself. "Well, in any case, that explains why I didn't expect to breakfast with company this morning."

Bradwell speared a rasher of bacon and egg and consumed it with every indication of relish. "But more seriously, Miss Cherwood, how do you think Mamma will go on now? Has the party truly set her back?"

"She is better—O lord, *far* better than when I first came to Broak. But she's so tiresomely headstrong! I *will* read my letters and I *won't* wear my spectacles, and I *shall* sit in the sunlight. I had as lief argue with an obstinate five-year-old. The doctor says that if she will only take proper care of herself she will mend very quickly. And honestly, the progress she has made—it's beyond anything."

"Should I try to scold her? I feel rather foolish doing so; she turns it against one, you know. Yesterday, when I suggested that she lie down for a spell, she told me she had no intentions of taking orders from a man she knew in his diapers!"

"O yes, I know about *that*—" Rowena began, but Bradwell had risen to his feet again as Margaret entered the room. After seating her, he helped her choose her breakfast, serving her with more eggs, toast, bacon, and tea than she could ever have hoped to consume in one sitting. Margaret thanked him prettily, altogether unaware of this preferential treatment, and Rowena, sitting forgotten across the table, watched with amusement, sparing a pitying thought for the absent Ulysses Ambercot.

"And what do you intend to do today, Miss Margaret?" Bradwell asked solicitously. Margaret looked expectantly at Rowena.

"I hadn't thought. That is, if Lady B—your mamma—wishes to sleep today—well, I had hoped there might be some sort of chore about the house that I could do."

"Such as what, goose? Polish the bannisters? Black the kitchen range? Mend the drawing-room curtain where that fat gentleman stepped through it last evening?"

"That's just it, Renna. I've no idea what one *does* in a great house if one is not a servant or in the nursery being fitted for dresses. Mamma talks of housewifery, but she never explains a thing."

"Whereas my mamma never talked of it, but showed me constantly how to manage a household. Mrs. Coffee and her people have the house well ordered now, though. What would *you* like to do? For once I am free of those odious lists and arrangements, and I can spend some time with you. Shall we descend to the kitchen and cast Cook out, and make some sort of mess ourselves?"

Margaret looked a little startled at this original proposition, and Mr. Bradwell downright sceptical. "You mean, truly cook something?" Margaret asked, and:

"Toss Cook out of her kitchen? Sooner face the dogs of Hades, Miss Cherwood," Mr. Bradwell admonished.

"Well, I have no doubt that the Regent is not going to hire me away from your mamma apurpose to set me up in his kitchens," Rowena agreed sedately. "But I can cook any number of dinners and pastries. There were times when we could not rely upon local people to help us, let alone maid or cook for us, and sometimes, while Mamma was arguing with the poulterer in what *she* called Portuguese—though none of the people *ever* understood her—I would make supper, and Mamma and Senhor Algues would make up over the dinner."

"Very picturesque, Miss Cherwood; you really have lived a rather unconventional life." It did not sound as if Mr. Bradwell was particularly interested in Rowena's unconventionality; he turned to smile at Margaret again. "Would you mind"—the question was obviously aimed at the younger woman—"if I made myself a part of your party? I don't think I've been below-stairs here since I was fourteen and hiding from my father's wrath over some trifling thing."

It was Rowena who answered, assuring him that he was more than welcome, and suggesting that they reconvene in the hall at one o'clock. "That will give me time to discuss things more completely with Mrs. Coffee."

All three were agreed. Rowena, with a backward glance and a certain feeling of pity for Ulysses Ambercot, unable to defend his interest, left Margaret to an absorbing discussion of nothing in particular with Mr. Bradwell.

Lady Bradwell, Miss Cherwood was informed, was fast asleep, and likely to remain so for some hours to come. After a short confabulation with Mrs. Coffee, Drummey, and the cook, Rowena was able to retire to her own room and change into a plain round gown which would not show the fatigues of an afternoon spent in the kitchen. The clock was striking one when she came down the stairs; Margaret was waiting, and Lyndon Bradwell joined them not a minute after.

Descending into the well-ordered cavern over which ruled Mrs. Teggetbury, familiarly known as Cook, they found only Amy, the scullery girl, and Susan-Amelia, her sister, who were comfortably settled shelling peas for dinner. Both girls jumped to attention at this unexpected appearance by folk from abovestairs, and even Rowena's assurances that they were not to trouble themselves could not bring the girls to relax. Finally, Miss Cherwood requested of Amy a general idea of where the stores were kept, and released the girls to play blindman's buff in the kitchen garden. Bradwell, with an amused appreciation of this scene, asked Rowena what had possessed the chit to start and stammer as she had.

"They've probably never been spoken to by one of the family, Mr. Bradwell. When Mrs. Coffee deigns to talk to one of them, that's probably as close to the 'upstairs' as either of them has been. Come along, Meggy." She applied to her cousin. "What would you like to make?"

Margaret, so applied to, could thing of nothing, but when Mr. Bradwell suggested that he had always been fond of ginger nuts, she readily seconded the notion. Rowena, on her part, professed herself disappointed. She had been hoping for a test of her mettle. "But if it's to be ginger nuts, then take this"—she handed him a vast apron—"so that you do not spoil your coat, and you may crack nuts and grate coconut and ginger for us." Margaret was assigned to the task of Cook's helper, outfitted with a similarly huge apron, and darted about discovering bowls and measuring trenchers. Rowena was stirring in the last of the flour, hands sticky with gingery dough, when Drummey entered the kitchen and coughed deprecatingly.

"Yes?" Lyn looked up from his chopping board, trying to assume a sober mien despite the disadvantages of coconut curling in his cravat and nut meats dusting his shoulder.

"If you please, sir, Mr. Ambercot and the Misses Ambercot have called, asking to pay their respects to the family and to the Misses Cherwood, sir."

Bradwell's face fell ludicrously. "Damme, discovered!"

"Well, oughtn't we to invite them in?" Rowena asked levelly. "After all, it would only be courteous, and truly, Mr. Bradwell, if you can stand the indignity of being discovered in your mother's kitchen, I would like to talk to Jane and Lully."

Bradwell frowned fretfully at Miss Cherwood. "I know nothing of your reputation, ma'am, but I misdoubt that mine can stand the ignominy of being found doing violence to this coconut."

"But if we leave now, won't that spoil the ginger nuts?" Margaret protested softly.

Bradwell cast her a speaking look.

"Cook would hardly hire you on as an apprentice scullrier, Mr. Bradwell," Rowena observed, glancing into the bowl he held. "But I see nothing to be ashamed of in your work here. And Lully and his sisters were always in our kitchen with me, and I with them in theirs, plaguing the life out of their very patient cook. In fact, as I recall, Lully was partial to ginger nuts as well; he will be quite handy as a critic."

"Very well, Drummey. Admit our guests," Mr. Bradwell said gloomily.

"Meggy my love..." Rowena grasped her spoon and began to stir the dough again. "That is a charming dress, and I wish you will not stand so close to the hearth. It will scorch that way."

Margaret obediently moved a few inches away from the fire.

"The Misses Ambercot and Mr. Ambercot," Drummey announced despairingly as he ushered the visitors to the highly unusual scene before them. To his privately felt disgust, neither Mr. nor Miss Ambercot showed the least dismay at their surroundings. Only Miss Eliza Ambercot made a great deal of fastidiously lifting up her skirts and showing a rather suprising amount of ankle. And close behind the visitors stumbled Lord Bradwell, looking for all the world like a sleep-ridden puppy absurdly dressed in cravat and riding coat. Every few steps his lordship would stop, shake his head carefully, and assume a puzzled air before continuing. Loud noises seemed to distress him.

"Damme, Renna, I might depend upon you to

turn the place inside out," Mr. Ambercot announced admiringly.

"I don't know why you say such a thing, Ulysses Ambercot, for I've done nothing of the sort. Do you still like ginger nuts? I require your opinion." Rowena held out a spoon which Mr. Ambercot, all unconscious of the threat to his pantaloons, obligingly sampled.

"First-rate. But it lacks something. One of those sweetish things—nutmeg or cinnamon."

These ingredients were sought anxiously, and when found and added to the dough, everyone in the kitchen sampled and opined upon it, with the exception of Lord Bradwell, who muttered that he was much obliged, and turned a pale green.

"Now, stop, or we shall have none for tea," Rowena demanded at last. "I hope you can stay?" she asked the Ambercots en masse. "And let poor Mr. Bradwell redeem himself by showing you how deedily he can turn himself out when he's not encumbered by Cook's apron?"

Lully, who had introduced himself anew to Margaret's notice (hardly necessary, as she had colored prettily, and followed him about with her eyes since his arrival) asked *her* if that was agreeable. Margaret eagerly assured him that it was, but added of course that her wish was nothing to Rowena's and to Mr. Bradwell's. And Lord Bradwell, too, of course. All their various encouragements were secured, and Margaret adjured not to speak such fustian, but to grease the pans which were to receive the sweets. It

71

required nothing more than that for Jane to remove her mitts and demand the butter and pans for herself, announcing solidly that she was due for a lark. Eliza watched distastefully: Even to catch Mr. Bradwell's eye she could not bring herself to mess with a bowl of sordid batter. It appeared that neither her brother nor the Bradwells found the project entirely beneath their notice. Eliza began to feel neglected.

The kitchen by now was the scene of general pandemonium; the unaccustomed nature of the exercise adding considerably to the hilarity of those involved. When the first batch of sweets was safe in the oven and the next laid out in tidy rows across the pan, there came a period of breathless anticipation, as everyone waited to see the product of their labors. Margaret, finding herself standing *very* close to Ulysses Ambercot, blushed deeply and went to sit by the fire again. When by Mr. Bradwell's watch and Rowena's eye the proper time was gone, it was Miss Cherwood who exchanged the first pan for the second, and placed the hot pan on the rack to cool.

Everyone pressed forward to look, since Rowena had strictly adjured them to leave the ginger nuts for teatime. Only Margaret hung back shyly and, when Ulysses Ambercot sent a glance in her direction, turned back to the fire so suddenly that, without noticing, the skirts of her muslin dress swept through the coals.

In a second the skirts were smoldering, then blazing. Margaret gave a terrified shriek and would have run from the room but for Jane Ambercot, who efficiently grabbed up the kitchen rug, and without looking to her own danger, wrapped Meg up in it and stifled the flame.

With a moan, Margaret dropped to the floor in a faint, and Jane fell with her.

Chapter 5

It took a moment for Rowena to realize that it was Eliza who was screaming; she moved toward the girl and struck her a quick, sharp blow across the cheek. Eliza retreated in sullen hiccups to watch confusion take over the denizens of the kitchen.

Everyone seemed able to move again—Lyndon Bradwell and Ulysses Ambercot moved forward at once, and would have scooped up both injured ladies to move then, but Rowena stopped them. "If one of you gentlemen will fetch the doctor as quickly as possible—thank you, Lully." She was fumbling through the shelf Amy had pointed out as Cook's personal place, discarding an empty gin bottle, a tuppence broadside, and came upon a bottle filled with a green, oily substance. Sniffing it once, she turned to the victims. "Mr. Bradwell, will you fetch some a blanket or two, and tell Mrs. Coffee I shall require her? And bandages, too." The tone and words were polite, but the voice one of absolute command, and Bradwell was suprised to find himself obeying instantly. "And Lord Bradwell..." she spoke to him sharply, for he was looking stunned, and greener than before. "Will you take Miss Eliza up to the morning room, please?"

Lord Bradwell acceded a trifle dazedly, and shepherded the still-shaking Eliza from the room. By the time Lyn Bradwell returned to the kitchen Miss Cherwood had liberally treated all the burns that she could reach with Cook's marigold-oil salve. Somehow both Margaret and Jane were taken to chambers abovestairs, where Lyn Bradwell found himself completely redundant and unhappily joined his brother and Eliza Ambercot; Mrs. Coffee and Rowena bandaged the girls as best they could and put them to bed.

When Dr. Cribbatt arrived half an hour later, escorted by a nearly frantic Ulysses, he found the situation much in hand. Jane's hands had been rather badly burnt, and the pain was such that he immediately produced a sedative draught to augment Mrs. Coffee's tisane. As for Margaret, the doctor at first had grave fears for her, and said that in the least he expected her to be badly scarred. A little closer inspection, however, and consideration of what restoratives were available for such a case, made his prognosis a little more optimistic. The burns were not so extensive as he thought at first, and in the main were less severe than he expected; with attention and rest, Miss Margaret might avoid being seriously marked. He expressed dismay that such a dreadful accident had come of mere foolishness, prescribed a powder, laudanum, and frequent application of the marigold salve (with perhaps a touch of gillyflower or crushed wheat kernel in the preparation), and left, promising to return the next day, or to send his assistant, Greavesey.

After seeing the doctor to the door Rowena went in search of the rest of the party. Lord Bradwell had retreated to the gun room, and even the news that the ladies stood a good chance to recover did not improve his harried, shocked look. Mr. Bradwell and Mr. Ambercot, however, expressed their relief feelingly, and even Eliza, sipping tea and murmuring softly about her poor nerves, professed herself delighted that poor Jane and Miss Margaret Cherwood would be all right.

"Of course, Jane ought not to move for a few days. Mr. Bradwell, do you think your mamma will mind...?" She trailed off.

"What a ridiculous question. You know Mamma as well as I do, Miss Cherwood."

"I shouldn't like to exceed my authority, Mr. Bradwell," Rowena countered gently. "And Margaret—well, she will be laid up for several

77

weeks at least, I'm afraid, but it seems that luckily I did the right thing in applying Mrs Teggetbury's salve. And now, I am going to look in again on both of them, and see if Lady Bradwell is awake. If you will excuse me?"

"Rowena, for God's sake, take care of her," Ulysses murmured fervently.

Leaving the room, Miss Cherwood was unsure whether it was his sister or Margaret he meant.

Once assured that her patients were sleeping as deeply as laudanum and their injuries would permit, Miss Cherwood went to look in on Lady Bradwell. Far from being asleep, Rowena's mistress was sitting up, fired with curiosity and extremely irritated that no one had thought to advise **her** of the calamity—whatever the calamity **was**.

"Hadn't you thought to ring and ask, ma'am?" Miss Cherwood inquired mildly, after Lady Bradwell had done ringing a peal over her.

Lady Bradwell assumed a face of injured virtue. "I didn't want to *trouble* anyone." She sighed heavily. If she had hoped to dismay Miss Cherwood with this pronouncement she was disappointed. Her companion smiled a little ruefully and settled herself on the foot of the bed.

"Well, to tell truth, Lady B, it's been sixes and sevens with us all this afternoon, and I did hope you'd sleep off last night's fatigues"—Lady Bradwell sniffed ungraciously—"before I had to trouble you with today's disasters. I'm afraid you will have to surrender your invalid's title for a while, ma'am. And worse, it really is my fault." Rowena proceeded to tell her employer, in terms as level and undramatic as possible, just what had transpired in the kitchen.

"Neither one is in danger?" Lady Bradwell asked at last.

"The doctor swears that with proper care both of them will be right as tops in time. Jane's burns are not too serious, although she sustained a shock. She'll be wearing mitts for some time, I'm afraid. Poor Margaret—God, ma'am, I don't know if I shall ever forgive myself. If Jane Ambercot hadn't acted to save her—I shall never forget that scene if I live to be ninety. I blame myself. If I'd not suggested that stupid game of making cakes in the kitchen—"

Lady Bradwell would not allow her the luxury of self-reproach, however. "And if I had not gone to give Katie Lester's child that blanket I should not have caught the scarlet fever that was in the village, and you would not be here at all, let alone messing in my kitchen, so the whole affair becomes entirely *my* fault. Silly child. Now, Rowena, I wish you will take yourself to your room and lie down for a while. And stop your fretting. It won't do any good, and the Lord knows, with me only half on my feet, we cannot afford to having you working yourself into the vapors. Now go on," she commanded briskly. "I vow I shall not worry you by reading in the dark or staring at the sun for half an hour on end. *All* your patients are abed, Renna. Do you get some rest as well. And tell Lyn and Jack that I shall dine with you all this evening."

"Very well, ma'am. I think Mr. Bradwell may be along to see you sometime later, in any case."

"Send him along. And I wish you will call him Lyn, my dear," the lady admonished from her bed, sinking again into the pillows.

Rowena, musing that her address of the prodigal son of Broak Hall was certainly the least of her problems, gently shut the door and returned to the library. Lyn Bradwell was alone, making a poor attempt to read the sporting papers.

"Ambercot went off to inform his mother that Miss Ambercot would be all right, and staying here for a short time," he informed her. "And, I collect, to counteract Miss Eliza's hysterics as best he might. Aside from the manner of a Tunbridge dowager, the chit has a habit of *clinging*. She's thrown a dreadful crease into the sleeve of this coat." He smiled, a little wanly, and flicked at an imaginary crease with one finger. "That *was* meant to be a pleasantry, you know,"

"Thank you," Rowena answered gently, and dropped with no further ceremony into a chair. "How do the invalids go on?"

"They're fast asleep, which Dr. Cribbatt insists is the best thing for them. And your mother wished me to tell you that she will dine downstairs with you this evening. And if you wish to go up and see her—" Rowena left the suggestion hanging.

"I collect you have already told her it was my intention to do so?" Bradwell asked dryly.

"Do you mind, sir?"

"Of course not. Thank you for reminding me, in fact. For a—" He hesitated.

"For a Managing Female?" Rowena suggested helpfully. Bradwell had the grace to blush as he continued.

"For a Managing Female, if you insist, ma'am, you are a remarkably able manager, and a light-handed one, too. In most cases."

"For shame, Mr. Bradwell, just when I was prepared to accept that as a compliment, however ill phrased!"

"Come now, Miss Cherwood. You took charge with the air of a sergeant-major in the kitchen—and a very good thing, as the rest of us loobies were completely unable to move." He poured a glass of sherry from a decanter at his elbow and offered it to her. "You do seem a trifle young to have developed that air of authority."

"Years of following the drum gave me an excellent training. But I think I assume my sergeant-majority only when it seems that's all that's left to do. Certainly, what I wanted to do in the kitchen was sit down on the floor and cry, or scream as Eliza Ambercot was doing. Which would have been very little to the purpose. And after all, it was my notion to mess about in the kitchen." Again, remorse growled in Miss Cherwood's lowered voice. "My cousin and Jane Ambercot lying upstairs, all for the sake of ginger nuts for tea!" She spilled a drop of sherry on her dress. "Damn!" she said and gave assiduous attention to rubbing at the spot. Bradwell tactfully ignored both the slip of her tongue and the tremor in her voice.

"Poor Miss Cherwood," he drawled at last. "You've been so busy handling everyone else's hysterics you've had no time for your own."

"Nonsense," Rowena countered a little more briskly. "I verily thrive on adversity, Mr. Bradwell."

Before Lyn Bradwell had a chance to dispute Rowena's statement, the door opened barely a hair's width and Lord Bradwell was peering around the door. "Are they gone?"

"Lully and Eliza? Yes, certainly my lord. Come in and take a glass of sherry for your nerves," Rowena offered kindly.

"Thank you." He breathed definitely. "It—O damme, I might as well be blunt. Miss Ambercot, Miss *Jane*, that is. Is she going to be all right? She don't give two figs for me, but I—I used to be, well, rather fond of her. Like a brother, you know. Still am. She'll recover?" However unremarkable this speech might have sounded to an inexperienced ear, both Mr. Bradwell and Miss Cherwoood were aware that coming from Lord Bradwell it was practically a declaration. His face turned a fiery red, while his brother's mouth twitched wildly and Miss Cherwood fought a smile which threatened to enlarge into quite unbecoming laughter.

"Certainly she will, my Lord," she reassured him. "But—"

"But?" he prompted.

"Well, when she awakens, we must all of us strive to keep her, and my cousin, well amused. It's very important to the healing process, you know. If you and Jane shared some common interests,—horses perhaps?—it would be a kindness in you to chat with her now and again to keep her spirits up. As a *brother* might."

"O, yes, well," Lord Bradwell stammered blankly. Then, after a moment's consideration, "Why, yes, I s'pose I could do something of the sort. Good idea, Miss Rowena. Very good idea."

"I'm glad you find it so, my lord. Now, if you gentlemen will excuse me, I have promised your mamma that *I* would lie down for a while myself. I trust I shall see you at dinner."

Miss Cherwood sailed from the room, her spirits a little lightened. She did not see Mr. Lyndon Bradwell raise his glass to her departing form with an appreciative smile on his lips.

To say that Ulysses Ambercot became a frequent visitor at Broak is to do him an injustice. From the morning following the accident Mr. Ambercot became so frequent a visitor that once, meeting him in the hall, Lord Bradwell was heard to observe that they had as well set up a cot in the pantry if Ambercot meant to keep cheering the sickroom party this way. In fact, Ulysses' visits to his sister, while most dutiful, were also remarkably brief. While he was determined to stay and amuse her, Jane was likely to cast him out after half an hour, saying that his fidgeting would drive her to distraction. He then would remove to Margaret Cherwood's room. Meggy was in considerable pain still, and relied greatly upon the doctor's laudanum draught to ease her discomfort. Still, she smiled sweetly on Mr. Ambercot no matter when he appeared, and told him when he left that he had made her forget her woes for a while. She did not seem to find his fidgeting unbearable, and with such encouragement it is hardly extraordinary that Mr. Ambercot would find greater and greater pleasure in her company. Often Rowena would chase him out with ridiculous threats, to Margaret's amusement. Ulysses was unaware that Miss Cherwood would be sternly upbraided by her young cousin for treating the visitor in such a fashion once he was out of earshot.

"If you can complain at the way I treat Lully Ambercot, you must be mending." was all Rowena would say to the matter.

"But Renna, he is your friend," Margaret insisted.

"And your admirer, goose. But Meg, love, if you expect to heal in time to catch him, you must rest sometime. And you don't want Lully to become *too ennuyé* with your company, do you?"

Margaret protested weakly, but her heart was plainly not in the denial. "Do you mind, Rowena? I mean, he *is* your friend."

"He was my playmate ten years ago, Meg. And if he were to offer for you and you accept him, I would wish you both very happy, and that's the end to it. Had you been imagining some unrequited romance between the two of us? Faugh. Aside from which, think how delighted you will make me if Aunt Dorothea reacts the way I expect her to, should you betroth yourself without her explicit consent."

"I couldn't do that!" Margaret said in tones of shock.

"If Lully applied to Uncle Cherwood and he gave his consent?" Rowena suggested. "Only what then would your mamma do with her precious Lord Slyppe?"

Margaret giggled. "Wait until Susannah is old enough to offer him!" she replied, cheerfully sacrificing her younger sister. Rowena, watching the younger woman laugh, a little painfully, thought that Ulysses Ambercot's presence and this same laughter were probably doing as much as Mrs. Teggetbury's salve and Dr. Cribbatt's sedatives to speed her cousin's recovery.

The person Rowena found herself wondering about was Lyn Bradwell. His interest in Margaret had been quite open on his arrival, and he was a dependable visitor to both the sickrooms, telling Margaret and Jane stories so outrageous that one or the other was bound to protest that he was bamming them shamefully. After the first week in the sickroom, Jane fell into the habit of spending the days with Margaret, so a visit to one became a visit to both. Mr. Bradwell's manner to both Margaret and Jane was friendly and courteous, albeit a trifle amused. Rowena entertained the notion that perhaps he had simply given up hopes of Margaret in the face of Lully Ambercot's persistence, or he was hiding a hurt beneath his facade of good humor and good manners.

"All of which is nothing to me, in any case," she told herself sternly, and went to consult Mrs. Coffee about the orders for tallow and wax candles.

Eliza Ambercot and her mother were frequent visitors too, often driving over with Ulysses to spend an afternoon. Anne Ambercot would usually stay a while in the invalid's room, visiting with her daughter and the girl she began to hope to have as daughter-in-law. Margaret, blissfully unaware that she was being passed upon, exerted herself to be pleasant to Ulysses' mother (insofar as she *could* exert herself, flat upon her back and still swathed in bandages) and found herself liking the lady extremely. But after an hour spent in the sickroom, Mrs. Ambercot was happy to refresh herself in the company of Lady Bradwell, stating that she was tired of forever stepping on her son, not to mention over Jack Bradwell. The two older ladies sat and gossiped leisurely over biscuits and chocolate; if having two invalids in the house to care for had returned much of her former energy to Lady Bradwell, having an old friend immediately to hand to talk and plot with very nearly completed her cure.

Miss Eliza, on the other hand, never seemed to be satisfied no matter where she was. If she visited Jane it was only for a few minutes, for

Jane would tire of her flutterings and airs, and ultimately would dismiss her. Then she would flutter over to Margaret, where the good-humored Meg would listen to her for an hour rather than send Ulysses' sister away. Usually, it was Lully himself who sent Eliza off, recommending that she pick flowers and stay out of trouble, which recommendation did not endear him to the heart of his younger sister. Again Eliza would visit Jane, in hopes that Mr. Bradwell might be there. After all, she reasoned, if that odious Margaret was taken up with Ulysses, perhaps Lord Bradwell or his brother would be found in Jane's circle.

Jack Bradwell very often was, as a matter of fact. Both Jane and Lord Bradwell, if asked, would have insisted that all they talked of was the stables, and indeed, as Eliza and Rowena could vouch for, most of their conversation did seem to center about depth of chest, good hocks, and a showy coat. If Jane ever tired of the subject she did not say so, and if Rowena, Lyn Bradwell, Ulysses, or Mrs. Ambercot thought the conversation in Jane's corner of the sickroom remarkably limited when Lord Bradwell was a visitor, they were too well mannered to mention it. Eliza Ambercot most adamantly thought that the conversation was a bore, but knew better than to admit it. After all, Lord Bradwell was *Lord* Bradwell, as well as being *Mr.* Bradwell's brother, and a wise young lady took care of what she allowed the gentlemen to hear. Mrs. Ambercot, in fact, sometimes wondered why Eliza seemed to be somewhat more restrained in her manner of late; the answer would not have pleased her.

With her mistress more likely to be up and doing, Rowena found her position in the house somewhat changed. She still oversaw a good deal of the householding from necessity, since Lady Bradwell was not, despite her disclaimers, healthy enough yet to tramp up and down stairs with Mrs. Coffee, discussing the condition of the green hall hangings, or the plaster in the maids' quarters. But frequently Miss Cherwood was left with unaccustomed free time. She would not haunt the sickroom, feeling that Ulysses and Lord Bradwell should have some time for their unadmitted courtships. So, when Lady Bradwell had no use for her and nothing in the house required her attention, she was likely to take her paints and easel out of doors for a few hours' sketching. It was as she amused herself one afternoon that she was accosted by Mr. Greavesey: Mr. John Greavesey, doctor's assistant.

At their first meeting some months before, while he was delivering Lady Bradwell's drops, Mr. Greavesey had evaluated Miss Cherwood pretty closely, deciding finally that she was an attractive woman of none-too extensive means. Nothing else, he was sure, could account for her tenure as a lady's companion, or for her un-married state at the great age of seven and twenty. She was always elegantly turned out, but this Mr Greavesey attributed to a saving disposition and a gift for improvisation, no mean thing in a woman. She was, of course, a trifle high-spirited, but that, he felt sure, could be dealt with over the course of time. In short, Mr. Greavesey had quite some time ago intended Miss Rowena Cherwood for his wife.

He had not yet, of course, apprised the lady of the honor due her.

Mr. Greavesey was not a vain man, and realized that he might, perhaps, be said to lack certain points in the way of dress, perhaps even of etiquette. He readily acknowledged, when challenged, that his chin was too long, his nose too pointy, and his countenance too lugubrious to stir a beat in the female bosom. He would even admit to a slight odor of quinine and asafetida which clung to his person at all times. Still, he flattered himself there were certain advantages to his suit which would certainly weigh with a woman so reduced in her own circumstances that she had no alternative to paid slavery as a lady's companion.

Coming upon Rowena at her painting was, it seemed to him, the ideal time for him to practice the charm of address which he felt he had in abundance.

"Miss Cherwood!" he announced with originality.

Rowena regarded him with irritation. The man was standing directly in her line of view, smiling his particularly cadaverous smile.

"Good day, Mr. Greavesey," she returned with as little enthusiasm as she could decently exhibit.

"Well, well, the artist at work, eh? What a pleasure it is for me to see the very hand of the artist at—at—at—" he floundered, at a loss for a word.

"At work?" Rowena suggested unenthusiastically.

"Exactly!" Greavesey returned, undaunted. "Might I not see the painting?"

Reluctantly, but feeling a bit sorry for her brusque tone, Rowena motioned for Greavesey to approach the easel. She had a certain feeling of relief that at least it was not one of her better sketches. And satisfaction, since the doctor's assistant obviously could not tell a good from bad piece of work, and was *ahhing* ecstatically.

"A charming piece, Miss Cherwood. Charming!" he announced at last. "But then, I am sure you do everything in the most charming fashion. I am come with her Ladyship's drops, and the sleeping draught for Miss Cherwood." He patted his leather bag contentedly. "And the doctor suggested that I might look in on both the young ladies to see how they went on. Might I hope that you will accompany me?"

There were very few things Rowena would have liked less to do. But common courtesy, and a feeling that she ought not to leave Margaret and Jane to deal with Greavesey's presence undiluted, made her put away the block of paper and wipe briskly at her brushes with an old rag.

"You are all goodness, Miss Cherwood."

"Nothing of the sort. The light is failing," Rowena lied ungraciously. "I had as lief go inside now as later." It was a particularly graceless speech, which she regretted the moment she made it. Greavesey appeared quite unaware of her hostility, and chattered on impressively about his great responsibility to Dr. Cribbatt, and his hopes for his future in the profession.

"In a short while I must begin to think about marriage, my dear Miss Cherwood. After all, for what does a man rise in the world if not in order to enable himself to pursue the absolute bliss of domestic happiness?"

Good God! Rowena thought. "I have often wondered myself, Mr Greavesey," she said drily. "No thank you." He had reached out to take her paints and paper from her. "I prefer to carry them myself. I am perfectly able to do, you know."

"Of course you are," Greavesey agreed. "It is only one of the courtesies which any gentleman feels due to a woman of charm and breeding, no matter what her station." He gazed upon her with a particularly fatuous expression, and Rowena strongly repressed the urge to hit him. Something of her feelings must have been expressed in her eyes or mien, for he abruptly stepped back and changed the subject.

"Miss Ambercot does very well. I expect by the end of this week we shall see her leaving Broak. As for my cousin, I think she gains strength each day. Do you think that Dr. Cribbatt will be able to come out to Broak some time in the next week to see her progress?"

"I am certain he will do so," Greavesey assured her rapidly. "Of course, if his other duties prevent him, then it will fall to my happy lot to come to Broak. Happy Broak, where I am always afforded the chance for some delightful conversation! So condescending, so gracious! And of course, the opportunity to pursue these delightful chats with you, my dear Miss Cherwood."

Happily for Rowena, they were rapidly drawing up on the garden. She once again resisted the temptation to box the man's ears. "Well, sir, I am going to go and put my paints away. I will join you in the sickroom. Yes, I believe that Drummey can show you the way."

A little disappointed, but not daunted by his dismissal, Mr. Greavesey followed Drummey into the hall. As she took another direction to reach the workroom where she was accustomed to keep her paints, Rowena could hear Mr. Greavesey trying in vain to strike up a conversation with Drummey; of course that superior individual was much too conscious of his own dignity to engage in chatter with a man of Greavesey's cut. By the time Rowena made her way to the sickroom, Greavesey, rather chastened, was already half way through his interrogation of Jane Ambercot, and his amour-propre did not sufficiently reassert itself for him to do more than wish Miss Ambercot and the Misses Cherwood a very good afternoon.

Chapter 6

Two weeks after the disastrous affair of the ginger nuts, Jane Ambercot was informed that she could prepare to return to her mother's house. Strangely, this idea was strongly resisted by Margaret Cherwood, Ulysses Ambercot, Lord Bradwell, and even Miss Eliza Ambercot; after some consultation Jane began to feel that in truth it might be for the best were she to stay awhile longer—if only to amuse Margaret, with whom she was becoming quite close. Rowena on her part smiled obscurely when informed by Lord Bradwell that despite the advice of that damned nuisancy doctor, *he* felt Miss Ambercot still too frail to withstand the drive of three miles. She smiled, said nothing, and reported to Lady Bradwell that Miss Jane would be a guest with them yet another while.

"At Jack's expressed command? Rowena, you witch, I begin to think you might just pull it off!" Lady Bradwell crowed with delight.

"My dear Lady B..." Miss Cherwood defended herself laughingly. "What on earth can you imagine?"

"I imagine nothing, my dear," the older woman said flatly. "You have set yourself the task of reuniting Jack with Jane, and I swear that if I see them happily wed I will consider you a wonder-worker of great dimension."

"You flatter me, ma'am."

"And you take me for a numbskull, girl. Now, how does your cousin go on today?"

"The doctor has said that she may sit up this afternoon for a while if it is comfortable for her. She will take her tea from the sofa in her room, and we shall see how she does afterward."

"With Ulysses Ambercot on one arm and Lyn on the other, I make no doubt," Lady Bradwell said with satisfaction.

Rowena felt a small nudge of annoyance. "Probably, ma'am."

"Well, if she weren't such a sweet child, I should say that she was a very sly puss." Lady Bradwell eyed her companion surreptitiously. "Which do you think she'll have?"

"To be honest with you, ma'am, I believe there's no contest. She's been moon-mad for

Lully since they met. I hope—I do hope that Mr. Bradwell has not attached too much importance to Meg, for I fear he'll be in for a disappointment if he has."

"Would you tell him so?"

"Me? Why, ma'am, I am—as he has reminded me on several occasions—your companion. Even if Meggy *is* my cousin, what earthly right have I to speak to him on such a subject? I'm certain he would consider it a great impertinence on my part." Rowena busied herself in rearranging flowers by the bedside.

"What fustian! Renna Cherwood, in the months I've known you I have never heard you speak such nonsense."

"Nonsense it may be, ma'am, but Mr. Bradwell made it quite clear more than once that he considers me a Dragon, and a Managing Female, and that he feels I have the tendency to overstep my authority."

"*Lyndon* said those things to you?" Lady Bradwell inwardly cursed the stupidity of her favorite son.

"Yes," Rowena replied simply.

"Then he is an idiot, which *is* a shame, as I had always assumed that Jack was idiotish enough to account for the entire family."

Miss Cherwood chuckled softly, and Lady Bradwell allowed the topic of her younger son to die for the moment. She had every intention, however, of reading her son a fine lecture at the earliest possible moment. When she finally found him she addressed him not only on the subject of Renna Cherwood, but of Margaret Cherwood as well. His replies, all in all, were satisfactory.

"I'm afraid Miss Meg isn't interested in me, except as that amusing fellow who tells the Banbury tales of life abroad, Mother. The same as Jane Ambercot is, and if she and Jack don't patch things up between them by next week, I shall be extremely surprised."

"So Rowena said."

Mr. Bradwell flashed his mother a quick glance. "Well, then, I suspect that the Ambercots will be in for a double wedding, for Ulysses seems to have made a mighty impression on Miss Margaret."

"So Rowena said."

Lyn flushed. "Miss Cherwood has a great deal to say, doesn't she, ma'am?"

"When it's to the point, my dear. After all, I am still partly a prisoner in this room, and I rely on Rowena to keep me abreast of what is going on—under my own roof, at least. Which reminds me, Lyn: Did you say something to Renna about her—her place here?"

"O, that." A faint smile and a rueful twist to his eyebrow suggested that Mr. Bradwell had already repented of that conversation. "When I arrived here, Mamma, I met Miss Cherwood in the gardens, and I'm afraid that I was a trifle brusque and she gave me rather a setdown, and when I found out who she was I made a few stupid remarks.... Did she tell you of them?"

"Indirectly, the other day. Not specifically."

"In other words, you don't intend to answer me yes or no." Her son lounged back and regarded his mother with amusement.

"I mean precisely what I say, Lyn," Lady Bradwell said with asperity. "Do you imagine that she came to me with some tale of ill treatment? I suggested that she address something to you—a question or comment on one subject or another; I forget what," Lady Bradwell lied gracefully. "And she said that she was afraid you might feel she was presuming."

"Good God, of all the mutton-headed nonsense," he muttered.

Lady Bradwell said nothing.

"Very well, Mamma, I admit that I had no business taking a stranger down on my first night home without seeing first how the land lay with you and her. But I have apologized to her for that remark at least twice, and—"

"It's not the sort of remark an apology will erase, Lyn. I fear that Rowena thinks you dislike her." This was spoken with consummate disinterest, but Lady Bradwell watched her son closely.

"Dislike her? On the contrary, I rather admire her. Not that that's anything to the point, since she's nearly bit my head off half-a-dozen times since we met."

"Probably because you bit hers off first," Lady Bradwell suggested loftily. "I never thought my own flesh and blood could be so stupid. Well, I will leave you to speak with Rowena or not, as your conscience dictates."

"My conscience? Good Lord, Mamma!"

But Lady Bradwell remained unimpressed with her son's protestations. "I am going to dress for dinner," she informed him, and sailed easily from the room, leaving him to wonder just what his mother had been driving at, and whether Miss Cherwood had truly formed a bad impression of him.

Eliza Ambercot, watching romances springing up between her brother and Margaret Cherwood, and her sister and Lord Bradwell, was highly displeased by the current events at Broak. She had joined Lord Bradwell and Ulysses in urging that Jane not be taken home to Wilesby House in hopes that her own frequent visits to the invalids would attract Mr. Lyndon Bradwell's attention and favor. At first she had planned to focus her attempts on Lord Bradwell, who after all had the title and the main of the wealth in the family. His growing reattachment to Jane was clear even to Eliza's self-absorbed eyes, and she dismissed him at last, telling herself that even with the title he was stupid and could only talk of dreadful old horses. Jane was welcome to Lord Bradwell, if she really wanted him. It was, on the other hand, unfair—more than unfair, intolerable—that *Mr.* Bradwell seemed as infatuated by Margaret Cherwood as Ulysses was. Eliza, had she given the matter much thought, could have argued her own superiority to Margaret in looks, charm, and certainly in importance. After all, Margaret was the cousin of Lady Bradwell's companion (be she never so wealthy). Eliza was the youngest daughter of a tolerably rich country gentleman; her mother was the third cousin to a Duke. In Eliza's mind there was no comparison.

But proximity did not seem to bring to Mr. Bradwell's attention the manifest charms of the younger Miss Ambercot, and the younger Miss Ambercot was losing patience rapidly.

Drawing on the advice of acquaintances she had made in Bath, with whom she had spent many hours earnestly considering the tactics of the Marriage Mart, Eliza considered her alternatives. She could give up her plans for Mr. Bradwell's future happiness and her own; that was ridiculous, plainly. She could wait, quietly, until Mr. Bradwell realized that Margaret and Lully were in hopeless case over each other and that Margaret was unlikely to spare him even a smile. That was a pretty tactic, but a little too uncertain and slow for Miss Ambercot's taste. She could, on some pretext, bring Margaret's tendre for Ulysses to Mr. Bradwell's attention and hope that on reflection he would come to understand Eliza's greater suitability. Or she could do something more direct.

Eliza had always been a partisan for the most direct approach.

Lyndon Bradwell was seated in the library writing letters when Eliza found him. She affected unconcern. He, after rising and bidding her good afternoon, returned to his work.

"What are you doing, Mr. Bradwell?" Eliza asked breathlessly.

"Composing a letter to my uncle, Miss Eliza."

"Oh." She thought about this for a moment. "And what shall you do afterward?"

He gave her a quizzical look. "I shall be writing to some friends of my uncle's, also in London."

"Oh. What are you writing to them?" she persisted.

"Business matters, I am afraid. Nothing that would amuse you."

Eliza took this setback in stride. After some idle drifting around in the room, she picked up a book (it proved to be a travel journal written by a very prosy old woman fifty years before). She regarded it avidly, and read not a word of it. When she was morally certain that she had been absolutely quiet for at least half an hour—that is, some ten minutes later—she stood, stretched, and wandered over to Mr. Bradwell's side.

"Still writing letters, sir?" she asked archly.

"Yes, Miss Eliza. Still writing letters. As I probably shall be for the next half an hour or more." His words were not unkind, but neither were they particularly encouraging. Eliza would not allow herself to be daunted by his tone, however, and inquired in a tone of awe what sort of business Mr. Bradwell was concerned with. He briefly answered that he was writing someone at the Foreign Office.

"I do not mean to be rude, Miss Eliza, but I

really cannot talk at the moment. It is important that I post these letters today."

"Oh." Eliza compressed a world of bruised but nobly hidden feeling in the word. Lyn Bradwell was not made of stone, and such a sound of mournful respect, issuing from a pretty young girl, made him feel he was every sort of monster of unkindliness.

"Wouldn't you be more happily engaged in talking with your sister or Miss Margaret?" he inquired with avuncular gentleness.

"They are taken up with other things," Eliza replied with dignity. Lyn had no trouble in guessing from this that Jack was talking stables with Jane, and Ulysses probably amusing Margaret with some sort of foolishness. Of course Eliza must have felt *de trop*.

"You know, Miss Eliza, that they mean nothing by it."

"O, it's nothing to *me,* Mr. Bradwell," she assured him. "I had by far rather sit here and be quiet with you." There was a slight emphasis on the terminal word which made Lyn suddenly rather uncomfortable.

"Indeed? Well, I thank you." He returned hastily to his letters.

Five minutes passed.

"Mr. Bradwell?" He looked up to find Eliza pratically in his lap, holding out a broken pen to him. "Do you think you could mend my pen for me?"

Fighting down a surge of irritation, Lyn took the pen and pointed it.

"Thank you so much!" She was effusive. "How clever men are!"

"Mending pens is hardly the exclusive province of my sex, Miss Eliza, nor an exercise requiring much cleverness. I dare say you could achieve the same result as easily as I." He returned the pen to her.

"O, no sir, not I," she breathed. "Perhaps some females might. Miss Cherwood, for instance; I fancy she could do almost anything. She's such a competent sort of person." In Eliza's mouth, competence sounded like a regrettable liability. After all, in her limited experience, only governesses, companions, lower servants and, of course, one's mother were competent at anything beyond watercolor and 'broidery—probably because these females were ancient, unattractive, and beyond the hope of attracting a gentleman's notice. Mr. Bradwell, however, did not share her view of the matter.

"Miss Cherwood is a surprising combination of ability, good sense, amiability, and—" He broke off, realizing that of all people he had no wish to be discussing his mother's companion with Eliza Ambercot. "She's certainly an admirable lady," he finished.

"And her cousin is so amiable too," Eliza agreed unenthusiastically.

"She certainly is." Bradwell turned to his writing table again.

"Mr. Bradwell?" She ignored the edge of finality in his voice.

"Miss Eliza?" A shade of exasperation crept into the polite words.

"Do you think it will rain today?" Desperately.

"No, Miss Eliza, I do not." Lyn stood and folded away his writing in the little desk. "If you will excuse me, miss? I've just recalled that I have an appointment in—in the stables." Making a perfunctory bow Bradwell left the room before Eliza could claim his attention again.

She could not run after him, either to tease him for his company or to scold him for his abruptness. That would not be good tactics. Immediately Eliza dropped her travel book behind some cushions and left the library to seek out company—any company, even the unexciting company of her sister and Lord Bradwell. As she climbed the stairs she found herself wondering if Lyndon Bradwell was not as stupid as his stupid brother Jack. She was rapidly growing out of patience with the whole race of Bradwells, even if Lyndon *was* dreadfully handsome and Jack bore the title. In fact, she had very little patience with the Bradwells, with her own family, and very nearly none at all with the Misses Cherwood.

Jane and Margaret, seated in a small parlor off Margaret's sickroom, were entertaining Lord Bradwell and Mr. Ambercot, and the room was alive with conversation and gentle with laughter when Eliza entered. Both Lord Bradwell and Ulysses rose when she entered; she was settled into a chair, asked a few distracted questions about the weather and what she had found to occupy herself with, and then was completely forgotten. Margaret had been settled half-lying on the sofa, tucked round with blankets and pillows which made her dark, delicate prettiness more distinctive. Eliza saw with positive dislike that Lully had somehow possessed of her hand and was talking—almost murmuring to her, Eliza thought disgruntledly.

Lyndon Bradwell might admire ladies' companions, but he saved his smiles for Miss Margaret. Lord Jack hadn't two brains to rub together—so everyone said!—and preferred solid, prosaic Jane with her square figure and plain talk, to her sister. And Ulysses was taken in by that dreadful, insipid, scheming Margaret Cherwood. It was the stupidest thing Eliza had ever heard of, and the more she considered it, sitting forgotten in the room, the more Margaret's perfidy, her nasty, missish, deceitful, hateful behavior grated on her. Asked what crimes Meg had committed, Eliza could probably, at that moment, have come up with half a dozen, not the least of which being the possession of a peignoir with more lace than any Eliza owned (borrowed, had she only known it, from Lady Bradwell's maid Taylor).

It was not to be borne.

"Lully," Miss Eliza said ominously.

Mr. Ambercot, recalled to the larger world for a minute, looked at his younger sister with surprise.

"Lully, I should like to go home now."

"Certainly, puss. By and by," Mr. Ambercot assured her, and returned his attention to Margaret Cherwood.

"Lully," Eliza insisted. Had he paid attention, Ulysses would have recognized her tone: He had heard it several times before in his life, most notably at the time when Eliza threw a bottle of medicine at his head. She missed her aim, and the bottle smashed harmlessly against the wall, but the room had smelled revoltingly of horehound for weeks.

"All right, Lizzie, I'll be with you in just a moment."

"Lully."

He regarded his sister with amazement. "Come on, puss." He rose from Margaret's side and took Eliza's hand in a firm—authoritarian—grip. They left the room but went no farther than the corridor outside it. Closing the door behind them, Ulysses Ambercot turned to confront his sister.

"Look here, what the devil do you mean by it, hey? We shall leave in a short while—I don't wish to tire Miss Cherwood. Or Jane, either," he added belatedly.

"O, certainly not," Eliza hissed spitefully. "While I sit about with no one to talk to and nothing to do, you and that hateful Margaret Cherwood sit and make eyes at each other." Her voice rose. "You know, she's nothing but the companion's cousin, Lully. I don't care who Rowena might be, she's the companion's cousin, and a dependent here, and why you're wasting your time talking to her and listening to her stupid voice and—"

"Look here, Lizzie—" Lully broke in with a voice of steel. "Keep your voice down, you silly chit. I don't know what maggot's got into your hat, but you'd best watch what you say, both about Rowena and Miss Meg, for Mamma don't like to have her friends talked about in that fashion."

"Mamma! Mamma ain't even here!" Eliza squeaked. "And at least your stupid old Rowena *works* for her keep. Why, that Margaret Cherwood just came to visit, and not the family, either, and she's made a May game of the household with her starting that fire—I suppose you think she didn't *try* to do something of the sort to catch your attention? Why, I know her type of female! I've met them in Bath. She's set her cap for you, Ulysses Ambercot, and you've tumbled right into the trap. She's hateful, that's what she is. Hateful, hateful, hateful—"

Eliza's voice, rising to an hysterical pitch, was stopped, suddenly, by a slap across her cheek. Jane Ambercot stood by the door, ruefully holding a bandaged hand and glaring at her sister.

"Come on, Eliza, I'll give you some cool water for your face," was all Miss Ambercot said to her, but in a voice that boded no good. "Lully, you'd best go see to Margaret. We heard everything our sister said in there."

"I don't care," Eliza wailed stubbornly. "It's not fair."

"Of course it isn't, goose. Nothing ever is," Jane answered firmly, and took her sister's arm gingerly.

Ulysses peered around the edge of the doorway. Margaret was seated upright on her couch, her face pale and concerned.

"Is Miss Eliza all right, Mr. Ambercot?" she asked timidly.

"O, damn Lizzie—" he began. "No, I don't mean that. Yes, I suppose she'll be right enough in a moment. I'm terribly sorry you had to hear her, though. If I hadn't told you already that she was the most fatiguing little nuisance alive I'm afraid I should really have to apologize for what she said. As it is—but you know what it is. Not a scrap of truth in her." He spoke as lightly as he could. Margaret's eyes dropped.

"Is that what everyone thinks?" she murmured at last, haltingly. "That I'm a—what is it? A hanger-on? And oughtn't to be here? I thought it was all right when Renna talked with Lady Bradwell, and that perhaps I could help in the household somehow and *do* something to show Lady Bradwell, and Lord Bradwell, and even Mr. Bradwell, how much I appreciated their kindness. And then I had that stupid accident—but Mr. Ambercot, it really *was* an accident. I couldn't—"

"Set yourself on fire? Certainly you couldn't, and only a little nodcock like Lizzie would even hint at such a thing. As for being a trial to the

Bradwells, that's the stupidest thing I ever heard."

"No, it isn't," Margaret insisted bravely. She still had not met his eyes. "I could have stayed in my room and caused no one any trouble, and instead here I am, in a larger room, with all sorts of attention and the loveliest food, and Dr. Cribbatt visiting here almost every day. I must be the most horrible expense! I should have gone to my grandmother's, I know. This only proves—"

"Nothing," Lully said flatly. He was at her side now, and had knelt at the head of the sofa in hopes of making her look at him. "But if you really feel this way, there is an alternative you might consider." He paused to clear his throat.

"Yes?" Margaret asked distractedly.

"I *do* wish you'd look at me, Margaret."

She raised her eyes slowly, as if the motion were difficult.

"You might—hum. Well, could you think of being—uh—engaged to me?" It was out, and now Lully was the one who had difficulty meeting her eyes.

"Just being engaged?" she asked doubtfully.

"Well, I'd prefer that you do the whole thing and marry me completely, of course," he answered solemnly. "Of course, if you really couldn't stomach that, I wouldn't *insist.*" Busy regarding the carved feet of the sofa, Ulysses missed a leap of joy in Margaret's eyes, and then a slight, mischievous smile which passed across her face.

"But how would that help my position here?" she asked blankly.

Now he looked up, to find her smiling shyly at him.

"I was hoping you wouldn't make me explain that far." Smiling back at her, he noticed that he had somehow taken hold of both her hands. She watched him; he regarded her nervously. Without warning, both of them began to chuckle.

"O, come on, Meggy, don't make me wait." He implored her through gasps of laughter. "If— if—you don't care for me—" His voice settled into a more sober tone. "Well, send me about my business and I shan't bother you again. But I did think—"

"If you think that you like me half as well as I—" Margaret began, and was stopped when Ulysses so far forgot himself as to envelop her in a painful, but highly satisfactory embrace. It was not until Margaret let a small squeak of discomfort escape her that he released her, apologizing ferociously for hurting her, and reviling himself as the greatest monster on the earth.

"But how long, d'you think, until I can— hum—hold you without hurting you?" he asked at last.

"Well, as long as you don't squeeze me too dreadfully tight, I imagine it can't be very long."

"Margaret, *will* you marry me? I mean, do I have to wait until you're well again before I can ask? To tell truth, I don't think I can wait that long."

"Lully, you aren't asking me because you feel sorry for me, are you?"

"Not for that reason, nor any other that my idiotish little sister may have put into your head. I'm asking because I should dislike to end as a bad-tempered old bachelor of eighty, the terror of my family and the regret of every matchmaking mamma for sixty years."

"And you think I can help to avert that?"

"Margaret, little love." He looked squarely at her. "I think you are my only hope."

"O, Ulysses!" she breathed. "What an utterly perfect thing to say!" And was again taken into a strong, but very gentle embrace.

"And just think how you will put my Aunt Dorothea's nose out of joint!" Rowena's voice came from the doorway. "Congratulations, Lully, for *finally* realizing what I've known for above two weeks. I shall not excuse myself for walking in, children; if you *will* leave the door open—"

"And what is it you have known for above two weeks?" Mr. Ambercot asked interestedly, from over the top of Margaret's ear.

"That you two were head over ears in love with each other. I dislike to interrupt you, and I'll leave you to make your *au revoirs* in private—yes, you see that I do have some sense of decency. But Jane suggests that you take Eliza home as soon as possible. She won't tell me what happened, but it seems that Eliza is still crying, and Jane says—"

"Spare us what Jane says, and tell her that I shall take Lizzie home in just a moment."

110

"And in the meantime I should leave you to your wooing and take my intrusive presence elsewhere?" Rowena asked good-naturedly.

"Exquisitely put," Mr. Ambercot agreed.

"All right then. But remember, Lully, that you don't want to tire Meggy too much."

"And Meggy would like to make it known that she is perfectly able to take care of her own welfare," Margaret said with dignity, from a vantage point tucked into Ulysses' shoulder. "And that she dislikes to be spoken of as if she were in another room."

"Meggy is very right." Rowena sketched a curtsy in her cousin's direction. "I'll be up with your supper in half an hour, coz. That is, if you can think of anything so unromantic as food."

"Certainly she can. Your business is now to mend yourself as quickly as possible, sweetheart—" Ulysses began. By the time he had finished explaining the whys and wherefores, with satisfactory demonstrations of his concern, Rowena had closed the door behind her.

Standing in the hallway she smiled. Perhaps Lady Bradwell was right after all; this matchmaking business, when handled correctly, was a greater amusement than she would have thought. With a shrug she went to find Jane and the very *damp* Eliza, with word that Lully would shortly be ready to return to Wilesby House.

Chapter 7

It would be difficult to determine who was the more delighted at the news of Margaret's engagement to Ulysses Ambercot: Lady Bradwell or Mrs. Ambercot. Of course, Ulysses himself protested that his delight must take precedence over theirs, but he was immediately shouted down by the dowagers, and told to mind his manners. Margaret, who was privy to a great deal of this rejoicing from the vantage of her sofa, smiled and dimpled prettily no matter *who* was delighted, nursing a secret surety that no one could be as happy as she. Together with Rowena, Margaret summoned up the courage to compose a letter to her mother informing her of her engagement; when it was done Rowena regarded the document with pride and a touch of malice, remarking that *this* would put a crimp in her Aunt Doro's bonnet for sure.

"She can't object, surely," Margaret protested fearfully.

"Mind it? Lamb, if I know your mamma she will be *aux anges*—only furious that she had no part in engineering the coup!"

Jane Ambercot professed herself ready and willing to welcome her new sister into the family at any time, and she and Margaret were happy to spend hours closeted together discussing Ulysses' talents and vagaries. Both the Bradwell men congratulated him and felicitated Miss Margaret, and Lyn Bradwell privately assured a somewhat apprehensive Ulysses that there were no hard feelings cherished on the matter. Anne Ambercot rode over from Wilesby House practically every day, as much to gossip happily with Lady Bradwell as to further her acquaintance with her daughter-to-be, and privately assured Rowena that, short of herself, there was no one in the world she could better like for Ulysses than Margaret.

The only person, in fact, who was not delighted was Eliza Ambercot. The worst of it was, in her eyes, that she had brought it all about. While she was publicly all that was sweet and sisterly, in private she would have gnashed her teeth had she not feared for the effect of such a practice on her teeth. It was these Cherwood women, Eliza decided, who had caused all the mischief. With very little effort she found herself growing to hate the sound of her soon-to-be-sister's voice. As for Rowena Cherwood...

Suddenly Eliza began to recall ills done her in times past by Rowena. The fact that Rowena twelve years before had been rather less aware of her than of the stable boy, and much less likely to have deliberately done her a mischief did not weigh with her. And Lyndon Bradwell, who had treated her so infuriatingly on their last meeting, had taken to chatting quietly with Miss Cherwood after dinner until the tea table was brought in. Clearly, now that Margaret was to be treated, perforce, as a sister, her cousin was left to become the enemy.

Rowena was aware of none of this.

Jane had been at last released entirely from the sickroom, although her lace mitts still covered light bandages, but with an almost-sister to minister to, it was not considered strange that she opted to remain at Broak awhile longer. Lord Bradwell insisted that she was not fit to travel (although he offered more than once to show her 'round the stables: A short, refreshing turn in the close air and noise of the stables could clearly do her nothing but good, he reasoned). Mrs. Ambercot put up no resistance to her daughter's protracted visit; Lady Bradwell confided to Rowena that she and Jane's mother had made wagers as to when Jack would *finally* come to himself and offer again. Since Anne Ambercot was at Broak nearly as often as her son, and Jane was practically in residence there, it was not strange that Eliza should spend a good deal of time at Broak as well. It was not strange, but it was often awkward.

When Mr. Greavesey called one afternoon to deliver balm for Margaret's healing burns and Lady Bradwell's ubiquitous drops, he found no one on hand but Miss Eliza available to take them from him. After some pointed queries it was revealed to him that Jane Ambercot, Lord Bradwell, Miss Cherwood, and Mr. Bradwell had gone for a brief drive; that Miss Margaret Cherwood was fast asleep, and that Lady Bradwell and Mrs. Ambercot were closeted together, "talking of weddings, I suppose." Eliza finished with dissatisfaction.

"Surely you should be with your mamma, Miss Ambercot?" Mr. Greavesey observed in his first flush of disappointment in Miss Cherwood's absence.

"I am not a child, Mr. Greavesey, at the end of my mamma's leading string," Eliza informed him loftily.

"Well, it is a shame that Miss Cherwood is not available, since I most particularly wished to give her advice on the administration of this salve." Greavesey pouted.

Eliza's demon spoke for her: "Yes, I know she will be *dreadfully* sorry to have missed you...." Her voice trailed off suggestively.

"Will she?" Greavesey had no trouble in believing this plumper; it had been his opinion for some time that Rowena Cherwood would, given enough time, drop into his hands like a ripened peach.

"O, yes," Eliza assured him, warming to her subject. "Why, I—no, I ought not to tell you this—"

"O, Miss Eliza, surely—"

"Why, Mr. Greavesey, surely you know!" Eliza cried. "Miss Cherwood has been—but no, I mustn't betray a confidence. I know that there is *someone* she has a partiality for, and—"

"Dare I hope, Miss Eliza?" Greavesey had forgotten the medicine in his hand, forgotten the doctor waiting in the village for his assistant's return, had forgotten even the courtesy due a young lady. He sank into a chair and raised his eyes to meet Eliza's. Had he not been, as the younger Miss Ambercot assured herself, such a loathsome little toad, she might have had some compunction at this point about leading him on in this fashion. "After all, I have the promise in me to become something of a man of substance, don't I?"

"Certainly, sir," she assured him demurely.

"It is not every young lady who can boast of such a suitor as I," he continued. To this statement, at least, Eliza could not take exception (although he would not have been flattered by her agreement had he understood her reasoning). "And after all, delightful as Miss Cherwood is, she cannot have much by way of expectations except to continue in her present— o, very honorable, but somewhat depressed condition."

117

Eliza was a trifle baffled by this statement, which she collected referred to Rowena's employment, but again nodded confidingly. "Shall I tell her that you called, sir?"

"No, no, my dear young lady, pray do not give yourself the trouble. If you will direct me to the housekeeper or some other reliable domestic with whom I may leave my medicines?"

Given Mrs. Coffee's direction, Greavesey sprang up in a fashion startling in one of his cadaverous appearance and walked—no, strolled briskly off to locate her.

"Toad," Eliza muttered to herself when she was certain he was out of earshot. "They deserve each other!"

And, quite comfortable in the knowledge that she had sewn the seeds of considerable trouble for Margaret's cousin, Eliza settled in for a short nap.

Jane Ambercot protested, after the first five minutes of their ride, that she really could not stand to drive on such a glorious day—if she truly was not to be allowed to ride, perhaps they could walk for a while? Lord Bradwell seemed a little discomforted by the suggestion; it was plainly unheard of to him that anyone, particularly anyone with Jane's usual good sense, could actually *like* to walk when she might be driven in comfort. But Miss Cherwood and Miss Ambercot were being handed down from the carriage by Lyn, and Jack Bradwell realized there was nothing for it except to hand the reins o the groom and bid him return the vehicle to he stable yard.

"I call that very accommodating of your rother, sir," Rowena confided to Lyn as they tarted off along the roadside, "considering that e is obviously reluctant to take to his feet."

"I suspect that if Jack ever musters the courage to repropose to Miss Ambercot, she will have im walking a great deal," Mr. Bradwell replied n a low voice.

"Is that a bad thing?"

"With a tendency toward corpulence, I suspect that walking may be the very best thing n the world for my brother, ma'am. Do you hink he *will* come to the point?"

Rowena, smiling, reflected that since the accident in the kitchen there had been a considerable lessening of the formality between herself and Lady Bradwell's prodigal son. "How can you ask me, sir?" she answered at last. "Can I be supposed to know?"

"To hear Mamma speak of you, yes," he said n no uncertain tone.

"O."

"I don't mean that to sound derogatory, Miss Cherwood. But Mamma has been praising you o heaven and Anne Ambercot for your handling of Margaret and Ulysses!"

"And nothing I can say will convince her that I did nothing to forward the match, except to isten to each sympathetically. As a matter of act, I believe you are more to be congratulated as the author of that match than I." She waved

119

aside his snort of indignation. "Eliza Amberc
said something about an interview with you tl
other day, and I collect you were so disobligir
that she could do nothing to relieve her feelin
but throw a fit at Meg—Lully of course felt hir
self bound in honor to offer for her after that

"What?" Bradwell looked at Rowena blankl
"What in God's name is the chit—O, damm
I recall it now. I was writing letters and sl
wished to get up a flirtation or something." The
walked in silence for a few minutes while I
considered this. Jane, leaning on Lord Bra
well's arm, was listening with every eviden
of interest as Jack described improvements i
his shooting cages.

"I hope he does offer for her soon." Rowen
chuckled drily. "Jane should get some recon
pense for listening to that recitation!"

"Is that the only reason you can conceive
for her marrying my brother?" Lyn regarde
Rowena with something near dislike.

"Of course not. What a silly notion. I adm
he should not do for *me,* but all I meant w
that. After all, love oftimes adds a positiv
charm to the least likely topics—at least to th
listener who loves the speaker. Are you dete
mined to pick a quarrel with me, Mr. Bradwell'

"No, certainly not," he answered stiffly.

For a few minutes neither one said a wor
each apparently bemused. Rowena stopped t
gather a few primroses, offering some to Jan
and carrying the rest herself. Bradwell, watcl
ing her, wondered if she knew the picture sh

made, dressed in a peach-colored walking dress of jaconet over an ivory slip, her leghorn hat lined and trimmed with the same peach hue which framed her dark hair and vivid face; she carried the flowers in one gloved hand and bent her head smilingly to breathe their fragrance. Bradwell smiled himself, watching her, but when she turned to resume her walk at his side, his eyes dropped very suddenly to his boots.

"Miss Cherwood?" he began at length.

"Sir?"

"I think—well, I must make my apologies to you."

Rowena looked at him with some confusion. "What on earth for, Mr. Bradwell? Unless you've committed some solecism I'm unaware of, which I misdoubt."

"Are you unaware of anything?" he retorted. "No, I didn't mean to sound that way. But Mamma said that you were under the impression that—well, our first meeting was not exactly a fortunate one, and I was, I remember, rather crude in my words to you on that occasion—"

"Never tell me that your mamma has been refining on that for all this time!" Rowena said, altogether astonished.

Lyn flushed with irritation. "I'm not saying these things at Mamma's command, Miss Cherwood. I only meant to apologize if I had given you the impression that I disliked you, and to hope that I had not given you an ineradicable dislike of me."

121

Rowena, uncomfortably aware that he was behaving far better than she, curbed her unruly tongue long enough to thank him for his consideration. "Shall we be friends, after all then? We do share at least one common concern, you know." Obviously Bradwell could not fathom her meaning. "Your mamma, Mr. Bradwell."

"Are you snubbing me by becoming the perfect companion again, Miss Cherwood?"

"If I am becoming any such thing, Mr. Bradwell, I assure you that it is entirely unintentional. Only, I am such an *imperfect* companion that I fear I take myself a little too seriously at times. I apologize in turn if I have seemed a trifle touchy on the subject."

"Well, are you two done apologizing?" Jane's voice broke into a circle of silence that seemed to encompass Rowena and Lyn. "I'm afraid I am less up to snuff than I thought, and Lord Bradwell suggests that we return to Broak now. *I* think," she teased, arm comfortably linked with Jack's, "that he is merely afraid that I will have a fit of the vapors and he will have to carry me back to the house unassisted."

"In such an event, Miss Ambercot, I assure you that I would certainly do everything possible to lend him a hand," Lyn informed her with ridiculous propriety.

"And I should be delighted to carry your hat and parasol, Jane," Rowena added.

"No, but won't you run along beside the spectacle and fan me with my hat and threaten to go into strong hysterics?" Jane asked in tones of deep disappointment. At this point, Lord Bradwell regarded the three of them with a very unappreciative eye and denounced them as completely daft.

"Not at all, Jack. I can see you simply don't want to share the honor of Miss Ambercot's transportation with anyone else. I call that mean-spirited in a man and brother," Lyn complained bitterly.

"If it disappoints you that greatly, Mr. Bradwell, I can contrive to faint too, and leave you to carry *me* back to Broak."

"Excellent, Renna!" Jane exclaimed delightedly. "If these men do not behave themselves, I will walk ahead of you, and thcy may — "

"No, no, Janie, for who's to carry you when you faint away?" At last in the spirit of things, Lord Bradwell looked down at his companion with such warmth that Rowena found it difficult to believe that some sort of understanding did not exist between them.

"To answer your earlier question, Mr. Bradwell," she murmured up to Lyn, "I think that he must be very nearly on the verge of it now."

"The verge of what?"

"Of making your mamma a dowager in truth."

Prevented by the nearness of his subject from quizzing Miss Cherwood further on the topic of Jack and Jane, Mr. Bradwell wisely kept his own counsel, and decided to watch the goings on about Broak Hall more closely for a while: They threatened to become amusing.

* * *

Rather than the half-hour drive they had planned, the party walked for little more than twenty minutes, and thus, when they returned to Broak, Greavesey was in the process of walking his ancient mare up the drive toward the main gate and the road for the village.

"My dear Miss Cherwood, it is of all things the most fortunate that we have met!" he enthused. "Pray, let me return with you to the house for a few minutes, for I have—heruhm-ah—some things to tell you from the doctor." If Rowena was not delighted with this plan she managed to control her reaction fairly well. Greavesey fell into stride with her, and Lyn Bradwell, on her other side, watched the progress of their conversation straight-faced. Miss Cherwood, painfully civil, was obviously stifling a powerful urge to hit Mr. Greavesey. The physician's assistant, on the other hand, was exerting himself to be as charming and suave as possible. For anyone but the two conversationalists involved, it presented an amusing spectacle. Rowena thought she sensed a smile edging the corners of Lyn Bradwell's mouth, but was helpless to do anything but make polite, noncommittal replies to Greavesey's inanities.

At last, back at the house, she requested that Mr. Greavesey talk to her in the office, and led him through the house.

"Well, sir?" She turned to him after they had seated themselves and the door had been shut to preclude interruptions. "Is there something in my cousin's progress which should alarm me?

Or something about Lady Bradwell? You might have left a message with one of the servants, you know."

"But I would have been denied the sight of your charming visage, my dear Miss Cherwood," he began.

Rowena tapped her foot on the floor, striving for patience. "Mr. Greavesey, if you wish to please me, you will refrain from that sort of remark. I don't care for it in the least."

Obviously, Greavesey thought, the lady had decided to play the game of coy maiden. "Ah, you wicked thing, you seek to make me declare myself before you will admit your own passions—"

"My *what?*" Miss Cherwood, plainly thunderstruck, sat straight in her chair and stared.

"Well," he continued heavily, unaware of her interruption. "I am perfectly happy to do so. You must know that I have been quite deeply affected by you since our first meeting some months ago. Oh, how long have I hoped, waiting to see some answering spark in your eyes. And very pretty eyes they are, too," he added.

"Mr. Greavesey..." Rowena stood up, gathering herself. Any man less self-absorbed would have quailed before the fire in her very pretty eyes and the tone in her ordinarily humorous, low-pitched voice.

"In short, my dear, nay, my *dearest* Miss Cherwood, I have the honor—and I hope I do myself no harm in supposing that it cannot be altogether a surprise to you, nor altogether unpleasant—to ask for your hand and heart."

"Mr. Greavesey, I think perhaps we have misunderstood each other." Rowena spoke as clearly as she could, as if she were speaking to a very young child. "Flattered as I am by your kind offer, I am afraid that I cannot accept it."

"No need to feel yourself flattered, by dear Miss Cherwood. And if it is your great sense of delicacy which forbids you to accept my proposals, I wish you will not consider it. Surely, it would be to my advantage to marry a woman of property, but where my heart is engaged I cannot quibble over wealth or the lack thereof. What a splendid doctor's wife you will make! Can you not picture it? You know that Dr. Cribbatt has spoken to me more than once of the day when I will take over his practice, and when that day comes, dear lady—"

"When that day comes, Mr. Greavesey, I hope you will be married to the woman you deserve," Rowena said carefully. "But for now, I must tell you that I do not think we should suit."

"Miss Cherwood, you are—"

"Being sensible, Mr. Greavesey. I do not wish to marry you—I am certain that I would make you as miserable as..." Courtesy, even now, kept her from admitting just how odious he was to her. "Well, I simply do not think we should suit."

"Miss Cherwood." Greavesey's tone turned ominous. "Do I understand that your affections are already engaged?"

Lyndon Bradwell's image flashed briefly into Rowena's mind. She banished it sternly. "You may think that if you like, sir. Whatever you think, I am flattered by your proposal, and regret to give you pain, but: no."

"I beg you will recall your position, Miss Cherwood. Can you wish to dwindle into old age as a companion, even to so pleasant a mistress as Lady Bradwell?" His tone had become menacing, and he bent his body forward to punctuate each sentence with a thrust from his bony chin.

"Mr. Greavesey." The words were forced out from between tightly clenched teeth. "If you have anything to say to me on the subject of Lady Bradwell's health or my cousin's, I beg you will say it. But if you continue to refuse to believe my most serious replies to your—your question, I shall throw you out bodily, myself. And if I find that I am not equal to the task myself, I shall enlist the aid of the stable boy."

Greavesey sat back in his chair, blanching.

"Further, sir, I would advise you, if you ever make proposals of marriage to a lady again, *not* to use insults and threats as your main points of persuasion. Good afternoon."

The words were as final as words could be. Miss Cherwood shifted her attention to some papers on the desk (they were inventories of the linen closets, and under normal circumstances would not have held a particular fascination for her), and so obviously ignored Greavesey's further presence that he was unable, by the wildest sophistry, to persuade himself that she was being coy. Huffily he took up his cane and satchel and left the room.

"Good God!" Rowena sighed to herself, and laid her head down on her arms in a weak, half-hysterical fit of laughter. "O, good lord!"

Greavesey swept out of the house in a manner more suited to a Byronic hero than a balding doctor's assistant. He had left the horse by the front door, and was thus forced to walk clear around the house to reach the stable and his horse. Jane Ambercot, sitting on a bench in the garden, called out a civil good afternoon to him as he passed, and more from habit than anything else, he stopped to exchange a greeting with her.

"Are Lady Bradwell and Miss Margaret Cherwood doing well, sir?"

"Why, of course, ma'am," he answered blankly, looking into her friendly blue eyes and seeing only Rowena's angry brown ones.

"Well, I did hear you tell Miss Cherwood that you had matters to discuss with her, and I assumed—"

"O, yes, well..." Greavesey hummed uncomfortably. "And how do you do, Miss Ambercot? Hands quite mended?"

"Very nearly so, sir," she said matter-of-factly, and pulled at one of her mitts to show the wisp of gauze which was all the bandage she now required. "The salve you and the doctor gave us has worked miracles! I only wish I had such efficacious remedies to hand in the stables at Wilesby House."

Greavesey had taken the hand proffered him and, examining it, found it in a fair way to mending without a scar, but also found it warm, squarish, a little plump, and pleasing. He kept it in his own for another moment or two.

"Well, sir," Jane began uncomfortably, wishing that the man would release her hand and leave her. "I suppose that you must be anxious to return to your work, rather than sitting and chatting with me."

"O, no, dear lady." Mr. Greavesey's sycophantic tone was tinged with the romantic melodrama he had enacted five minutes before. "It is a positive refreshment to the soul to stand in this beautiful garden and talk with one so charming as yourself."

"Yes, well, sir, I thank you for the compliment, but..." She tried to pull her hand away. Greavesey seemed to be retaining hold of it less on purpose than because his attention was fixed elsewhere. Jane, thinking to bring him back to himself, gave the hand a gentle tug. His own hand closed tighter around it. "Mr. Greavesey?"

No answer was vouchsafed.

"Mr. Greavesey?" She tried again.

Again, no answer. His gaze appeared to be focused on the corner of her marble bench, and whatever he was thinking, he had tightened his grasp painfully.

"Sir?" Jane's voice was a little more imperative now. "Mr. Greavesey, I think I should be going into the house now."

"O, yes." He agreed morosely, but made no sign of relinquishing his prize. "Everyone has other things to attend to. *I* have other things to attend to. O yes, well, we mustn't mind about poor old John Greavesey; there are more important things to give our thoughts to, ain't there?"

His hand closed tighter still, and Jane cried out in pain. "Sir, you're hurting me!" He didn't seem to notice. "Mr. Greavesey! You're obviously upset about something, perhaps a cup of tea would—"

"Tea, dear lady? Tea? What's that to the purpose, I ask you? No, no one has time to spare a thought for John Greavesey, I tell you." Still the hand was clasped in his, although his grip had loosened somewhat now. Jane, still seated on the bench, stared up at him in uneasy dislike.

"Now, nothing of the sort, sir. If you will but release my hand and follow me indoors, we shall be pleased to give you—"

Whatever it was that Miss Ambercot was to have offered Mr. Greavesey, the words were lost as Lord Bradwell, come upon the scene, charged, rather like a bull, and with one solid left knocked the older man down.

"Take your hands off her, you—you—" Words, as usual, did not come easily to Lord Bradwell.

"Why, Jack!" Jane rose, her face reflecting a little surprise and much gratitude. She put out a hand, the one just relinquished by the now-flattened Greavesey, only to have it quite rudely pushed away.

"Don't you 'Why Jack' me, ma'am! Sitting in the garden beguiling yourself by getting up flirtations with a half-witted sawbones, is it? When I consider how once, long ago, I let myself be made ashamed for a little dalliance, and now I come on you in the garden with this bag of bones, and obviously enticing him by—"

"Jack Bradwell, what on earth are you talking about?" Jane appeared roused to a fury to equal his. On the ground beneath their notice, Greavesey lay and stared directly upward at this new melodrama.

"You know very well what I'm talking about," Lord Bradwell insisted. "And I don't mean to make a guy of myself by attending on a woman who would sit holding hands with that—that—that—"

But Jane, holding her hands in front of her face, did not stay to hear herself or Mr. Greavesey reviled further, and Lord Bradwell and his victim were left to stare blackly at each other.

Chapter 8

By the time Miss Cherwood sufficiently recovered herself from Mr. Greavesey's proposals
to emerge from the office, Jane Ambercot had
retired noisily to her room, announcing in an
uncharacteristically melodramatic way that
she would not see *anyone*. Jane's maid, much
disgruntled at being included in this ban, confided in Rowena that she thought she had heard
the sound of crying from her lady's room once
the door was closed. Little as she liked the situation, Rowena could not suppose that any purpose would be served in storming Jane's room,
so she contented herself in sending up a light

supper and hoping that a chance would come to talk to her friend.

Lord Bradwell, on the other hand, was very much in evidence at dinner and afterward. He stalked about the drawing room with a distempered sneer for anyone who approached him. The effect would have been ludicrous, except that he was so much in earnest that it was impossible to laugh at him. "For all the world like Young Werther!" his unhappy mother confided in her companion. "My dearest Rowena, what could have brought my sunny Jack to such a pass?"

"I imagine it must have to do with Jane, ma'am, but as to what the particulars are, I cannot tell you more than you know."

"Just when things were looking particularly promising. Well, had you managed to pull them through, I was hoping to delegate responsibility for Lyn to you as well."

Rowena started slightly. "I beg your pardon, ma'am?"

"I was going to ask you to try your matchmaking on Lyndon, dear. But with this experiment gone so awry..."

"I agree completely," Rowena said with alacrity. "After all, ma'am, I never claimed to be better than a very amateur at this game."

"I know it. But you seemed to show such promise! In any case, I'm sure that these silly clunches have brought themselves to whatever pass it is they've found, and I am minded to let them resolve it themselves," Lady Bradwell said disgruntledly. "After all, I have waited *years* for Jack to come to his senses, and just when he appears to be doing so—Faugh! And look you there at Lyn, talking with Ulysses Ambercot quite as if nothing in the world were the matter! And his brother walking about like a bear!" The older woman sniffed disparagingly. "Rowena, I warn you now, in case you ever consider marriage: Men are fools. They have their good points, and all in all I cannot regret having married Bradwell—" A soft smile lit on her lips for a moment and was rigorously erased. "But by and large, they are the most contrary breed imaginable!"

"Until you need them, ma'am?" Rowena suggested.

"Certainly, child. Until you need them. I didn't say they were useless altogether," Lady Bradwell replied with dignity, and applied herself to her teacup.

Whatever his appearance, Lyndon Bradwell was not in the least unaware of his brother's novel behavior. His good-natured attempts at conversation had been rebuffed with a violence he would have thought impossible in his brother, and somewhat later in the evening he talked to Miss Cherwood, hoping that she, at least, might have a clue to the mystery.

"After all, Miss Cherwood, you seem to be the confidante of most of the household; now what the devil has come over my brother?"

"And Miss Ambercot. I wish I knew, Mr. Bradwell. I should certainly like to find out."

135

"I wish you will; having Jack stomping around the house in a cross between a brown study and the rage of a bear—"

"A brown bear?" Rowena interjected amiably.

"If you like," he replied absently. "It's distracting. I've never seen Jack act like this."

"I think it may be love. I only wish I knew for certain—at least that would set your mamma's mind at ease."

"Is everyone in this household privy to everyone else's *affaires de coeur?*"

"I hope not." Miss Cherwood cast him a look of aspersion. "But I mean to find out what's afoot, and right it if I can. I'm sure that sounds abominably nosy of me, but if I've the reputation for it, I may as well get some good of it as well. I dislike seeing people so miserable. As you say, it is highly—um—distracting."

"So far from being nosy, Miss Cherwood, I for one would regard your intervention as a kindly gesture toward the rest of us. Damme, at least your cousin and Ambercot accomplished their wooing in a sensible manner."

"With that license, I shall go to see what I can do, sir." Rowena rose and made him a schoolgirl curtsey, then turned to take her leave of her mistress. Lyn, watching her, thought, not for the first time, what a remarkably graceful woman she was.

Margaret was almost asleep when Rowena reached her room, but roused herself enough to sit up, smile drowsily, and enjoy five minutes conversation with her cousin. Formerly all her discourse had been on books, family, clothes, and schoolroom topics. Now, every other phrase seemed to begin with the words "Lully thinks..." or "Ulysses told me ..." The time when she was not quoting Ulysses Ambercot's views on everything was filled with fretting about her parents' answer to Ulysses' formal request for her hand. "What shall I do if Papa says no, Renna?"

"Why on earth should he, love?" Rowena smiled at her cousin's distracted happiness and prayed that the letters from London would come soon, before Meg worked herself into a frenzy or bored everyone in the household.

It was asking too much to hope that perhaps Jane had confided in her fellow-invalid, and Rowena found no answers to that mystery with Margaret. At length she bid her kinswoman good rest, made a quick inspection of her wounds and, taking her leave, gathered her strength to approach Jane.

At first she was denied entry to the room unequivocally. Upon receiving Miss Cherwood's announcement that she would enter the room in any case, Jane rose up and let her in.

Tears are not becoming to any but the most ravishingly pretty, and Jane Ambercot was, at her best moments, no more than rather handsome. Now, with her face flushed, her hair in entire disarray, her eyes red-rimmed and her mouth trembling, she looked quite dreadful. Add to this that she was sitting bolt upright in her chair, hands clenched and face cold and withdrawn, and Rowena was sorely tempted to turn about-face and leave Miss Ambercot and Lord Bradwell to solve their own problems. Only a trace of loneliness and despair in Jane's eyes persuaded her to stay. She went to her friend's side, knelt, and put an arm about her waist.

"Jane dear, what on earth has made you look so miserable?"

"Nothing."

"Nothing? That's the greatest plumper I ever heard! When this afternoon we were all so cheery, and you so well? Tell me to mind my own business if you like—I shan't, of course—but don't try to bam me with such nonsense as that. I am not so green as I'm cabbage-looking, my girl, and though I be a veritable monster of inconsideration, I shall not sit by and see my friends miserable."

The concern under Miss Cherwood's rallying tone reached Jane as nothing else would have. The first of a new flood of tears stood in her eyes and she choked out: "I *hate* men. They're all stupid and egotistical, and selfish, and—and *men*." This was apparently the worst imprecation she could summon, and having spewed it forth she burst splendidly into tears and found herself weeping noisily on Rowena's shoulders.

Miss Cherwood took this all with near-perfect equanimity, producing a handkerchief she had provided for the occasion, and mopped Miss Ambercot's eyes while clucking comforting noises in her ear. At last, when both women were about equally damp, Jane found words to explain her distress.

"It was that odious man, the doctor's helper—"

"Greavesey?" Rowena lifted an eloquent eyebrow in amazement. "He *was* busy today, wasn't he?"

"I was sitting in the shade, waiting for Jack and he—not Jack, your odious Mr. Greavesey—he came by and I said hello. I swear, that is the only thing that I said to him, and I wish I had never been so civil in all my life! And what must he do but stand there, holding my hand—and a deuced lot it hurt, too, with him squeezing it!—and talking of how no one could spare a thought for poor John Greavesey! And feeling very sorry for himself too, I can tell you, and telling me how charming I was. I tell you, Renna, I have never been so eager to kill anyone in my life, only *then* I felt sorry for him, he was such a detestable little man. And babbling of tea and refreshments to his soul—have you ever heard anything so abundantly stupid in your life? No—I beg your pardon. I was the one who brought up the tea. But it was only because I thought that perhaps *that* way he would let my hand go—to come in for some tea. And perhaps then I could have asked you and Drummey to have him locked up safely until he could be sent to Bedlam!"

"When was this?" Rowena asked suspiciously.

"Not long after we returned from our walk. I suppose he must have just left you, and he was—"

"A trifle perturbed?" Rowena suggested mildly. "This all seems to be my fault, after all. Well, then, let's have the rest of it. What finished this little tête-à-tête in the garden?"

"Now you sound like Jack." Miss Ambercot said in tones of loathing. "It was *not* a tête-à-tête, and that stupid idiotish man—"

"I apologize. But what *did* Jack say?" Rowena pressed.

"He came upon us just as, I think, I was prevailing upon Mr. Greavesey to let go of my hand and come indoors. And he immediately accused me of flirting with that odious undertaker of a man, and stood there glaring at me as if I were the Fallen Woman of Babylon! And adverting to—well, an earlier time when we..."

"I know the whole of it, Jane. But he thought that you had set up the flirtation yourself? Lord, then this really *is* all my fault. You see, just before he met with you, Greavesey had been making his proposals to *me*. And there simply is no way to tell such a man as he is *No* without insulting him. And if you do not insult him, he thinks you are being coy and maidenly—yes, he even used those words. Can you credit it?"

"And from romancing you he came upon me and—"

"It would seem he was in search of solace. Well, at least I can explain that to Jack and—"

Jane sat bolt upright again. "No you will not!

Don't you dare. Rowena, I don't want anything to do with that man, and I forbid you to waste your breath in trying to explain anything to him."

"I was only proposing that I waste my breath because he is quite spoiling everyone's dinner—sulking and pouting in the most alarming way. It would be a kindness to Lady Bradwell, you know."

"I tried," Jane said with the simplicity of the wronged. "I tried to explain to him, and do you know what he did?"

"Blamed you for blaming him when he had his flirtation with the other female years ago, and compared the two instances," Rowena stated matter-of-factly.

"How did you know?"

"My dear, can you conceive of anything more obvious? It is the perfect connection for an aggrieved gentleman to make. Not only that, but I'll wager that by now, aside from the monstrous fine sense of ill use which he is nourishing in his breast, Lord Bradwell has very little thought for anything but how he can apologize to you for being unjust."

"Then he may nurse that for all he is worth," Jane announced solidly.

Rowena was silent.

"I want nothing to do with him."

Still Rowena kept her tongue.

"Renna, what would you do?"

"That depends, of course, on whether or not you truly never wish to see him again," she said consideringly. "I imagine that if I truly loved him, despite the fact that he had been abominably stupid, I would tell him what happened, enlist any others—such as myself—who could corroborate my story, and remind him when I was done that I cared for him. And then—but this is the hardest part—wait and see if he is truly a stupid, loathsome, horrid man, or merely human. If he's human, I believe he would eventually see reason."

"But why should *I* apologize to *him?* I'm telling the truth, aren't I?" Jane's voice shook with exhaustion and irritation.

"Of course you are, so you can afford to be a little generous. When he realizes that he has done you an injustice he will likely be extremely penitent. But do you think it's worth it to lose him over a matter of pride, Jane?"

This sobering thought evidently carried some weight. "No, I suppose not."

"Do you wish me to talk with him? Explain what was what with Greavesey this afternoon?"

No words, but a mute nod of the head signified Miss Ambercot's wishes.

"Very well, then, I suggest that you go to bed now. All this untamed emotion is very tiring, and I wish you will remember that you are only lately up from the sickroom."

"Very well, Renna."

And Miss Cherwood, conscious of a certain exhaustion herself, retired to her own rooms to think of the coming confrontation with Jack Bradwell.

* * *

She had planned to corner him in the office the next day, or very possibly in the stables, and had spent a good part of her dressing and washing thoughts on planning speeches to make to him. Instead, he took her unawares by descending earlier than usual to breakfast. He was there, tearing savagely at a beefsteak and drinking ale and coffee (thankfully from different vessels). He barely acknowledged her greeting. Lyn Bradwell, also in the midst of his breakfast, smiled warmly at her, cocked his head in his brother's direction as if to say "No luck here," and offered her the teapot. She was trying to frame a way to introduce the topic of Miss Ambercot into the conversation, but needn't have bothered: Lord Bradwell introduced the subject himself.

"How much longer can we expect to have Miss Ambercot in the house?" he asked in a deadened voice.

"Why, I think that is as much your mamma's decision as anyone's, sir. She only stayed to keep my cousin company and—" But it would not be good tactics, at least at this point, to remind the gentleman that he had specifically asked that Jane extend her stay. Lord Bradwell returned his attention to his steak, and Lyn's look conveyed his sympathy at her rout. Rowena tried another tactic.

"I wish one of you gentlemen might have a word with Dr. Cribbatt about his man Greavesey," she began calmly. Lord Bradwell's head came up and he glared at her. Rowena continued unheedingly. "That man—I don't know what to say of him! Yesterday afternoon he suddenly burst into a string of romantic nonsense and asked me to marry him!"

Both the Bradwell men looked ready to swallow their spoons in surprise.

"He did what?" choked Jack, and: "That funereal beanpole!" Lyn exploded.

"The same. I tell you, he was not easily dissuaded, despite the fact that I had given him no encouragement, and he left me in such a state that I truly wondered what he would do when he was gone! If looks could kill, I should be laid out in the chapel at this moment."

"Jane told you to say this," Lord Bradwell broke in angrily. "By God, why should I believe—"

"What has Jane to say to this? Why, did he disturb her peace too? Poor child, and she only now recovering her health. If I had had to talk to the man for another five minutes together, I think I would have hit him."

"Excuse me." Lord Bradwell arose from table and stalked out. Rowena had a moment's doubt as to the success of her strategy, but put her trust in the man's innate generosity, his love for Jane, and his deep lack of real imagination. Sooner or later, she was sure, the image of Greavesey pressing his company on Jane would overshadow, by its mere plausibility, the ridiculous fantasy of Jane enticing the spindly, lachrymose physician. After all, Rowena thought as she poured another cup of tea, what man would willingly believe that he and Greavesey were in the same class?

"May I have the scones, please?" she asked the remaining Bradwell politely. "You know, all this emotion makes one dreadfully hungry."

"Yes, it does rather." And she offered him the plate again.

What exactly passed between Jane Ambercot and John, Lord Bradwell is unknown, for neither one would tell any part of the story to anyone else. Margaret and Rowena both heard raised voices coming from Jane's sitting room, but neither interfered. And early in the afternoon, Lady Bradwell swept triumphantly into the office, cast her blue spectacles from her in an excess of glee, and announced the betrothal of her elder son and Miss Ambercot.

"Well, that's a mercy," said Rowena.

"Isn't it?" Lady Bradwell sighed and settled herself comfortably on the edge of a chair. "After all the years of work I put into the two of them, and then you are here not six months and they are engaged again! Renna, I believe I *was* right about you after all."

"That I'm a matchmaker, Lady B? Never say it, I beg you. I hate to see my friends miserable, it's true, and will go to some lengths to prevent it, but as for seeking out matches—"

"You may be as pragmatic as you like," Lady Bradwell shook her head and continued loftily. "I am delighted, and—O, Lyn, Lyn!" She waved a kerchief madly at the window, and Lyndon Bradwell's retreating figure stopped, turned around, and came quickly up the garden path to the door.

"Hullo, Mother. Miss Cherwood. What's to do, ma'am? And ought you to be so much in a flutter?"

"I shall be anything I like, boy, and you recall that I knew you in your diapers!"

"And before, no doubt. Mamma, what is the cause of this jubilation?"

"Rowena has done it! Jack finally stopped being a pudding head and has asked for Jane, and they're betrothed again."

"I had very little to do with it," Rowena insisted. "They'd have quit the quarrel very shortly, I'm sure. I only hate seeing Friday-faces about the house."

"A laudable sentiment, I'm sure. And I'm delighted too. But ought you to be prancing about in the sunlight, ma'am?"

"You are determined to be disagreeable and send me back into the darkness when I haven't the least wish to do so. Very well, I shall go, but I will be down for dinner, and Jack will make a formal announcement of the betrothal. And about time, too." Lady Bradwell finished defiantly. "Remains only you, Lyn."

"It does look that way," he agreed, and held the door for her.

"Well," Bradwell began as he watched his mother climb the stairs. "Happy endings seem to be the vogue. If Mamma appears at dinner to tell us that she and Dr. Cribbatt have decided to make a match of it, I shall not turn an eyelash."

"Disgustingly sentimental, ain't it?" Rowena returned to her desk.

"Disgraceful. I begin to feel very old and sensible, and shall no doubt spend the entire evening wandering through the halls murmuring 'Bless you my children' to all and any I meet."

"Well, the choice of words is yours. You probably could go about muttering in Spanish, or Russian, or gibberish for all of that, and I am sure your blessing would be gratefully received."

"In that case, I shall by all means try gibberish." He closed the door behind him and stepped into the room. Rowena, who had been working at the desk when Lady Bradwell had entered to make her announcement, regarded him with some surprise. Of course, he had been on his way somewhere when Lady Bradwell had hailed him, and he intended to go out again through the garden door. "Don't you find this bridal air a trifle fatiguing?" he asked, settling on the edge of the chair his mother had briefly occupied, and fiddling with a bit of pillow fringe.

"If you mean, shall I play the maiden aunt to match your depressing paternalism, the answer is no. I refuse to do."

"Refuse?"

"I shall certainly be an aunt soon enough, if the look in Lully's eye—and Meggy's too!—means anything. So I refuse to rush the season.

When the time comes, I hope I will make an admirable aunt, dispensing favors with sweets and affection in about equal proportion. Until that time, I am not going to let myself feel maternal toward a group of people nearly my own age—or in your brother's case, older. In fact, the thought that you feel like Lord Bradwell's father—or uncle or whatever—is far and away the most Sophoclesian thing I have ever heard." Conscious of the fact that she was, to her own ears at least, running on absurdly, Rowena stopped abruptly.

Lyn seemed to consider this. "It would be a dreadful waste, you know."

Rowena made of that what she could.

"Meg and Ulysses? I had hoped that you wouldn't feel that way; you know you would not have suited each other. Not that that makes a difference when one has a tendre—"

"That wasn't what I meant, Rowena."

With his use of her name the atmosphere in the room changed from the light-headed froth of Rowena's teasing to something unsettled and decidedly disturbing. She found that her heart was beating rather erratically.

"You of all people shouldn't dwindle to maiden aunt. Not that you'd dwindle, of course. And you'd certainly make an admirable aunt, almost as admirable as you'd make a mother. And that, almost as admirable as the wife you'd make."

"What a pity there weren't more men of your opinion when I appeared in London last," Rowena said, attempting a lightness that she was far from feeling. She had left the desk and stood now by the book case, aimlessly running her eyes over the shelves.

"Some people don't know quality when they see it," he began lightly. Stopped. Seemed to have come to a decision. "Rowena, I don't want to go through the same charades that Jack and Ulysses have been through in these last weeks. I keep feeling there must be a better way to ask—" He looked at her, a look strong enough to gather her startled attention from the books, from the window, from any other object in the room, and fix it firmly on his face. "Marry me, Rowena?"

With what seemed like immense effort she smiled. "Mr. Bradwell, this is so sudden." Her voice was dry, her smile unconvincing. More firmly she managed to say: "Lyn, are you simply trying to keep in step with the matrimonial air of the household? Jack and Jane—"

"To hell with my brother and Jane," he said succinctly.

"Or is it because of Meg? I really don't fancy being someone's justification, or solace, or what-ever—"

"What about my wife? It's all I asked of you. And you would do me a great kindness if you would disabuse yourself of the notion that just because your cousin is a pretty chit and I have an appreciative eye—yes, I'll tell you that now, for you'd best adjust to it!—that I was madly in love with her."

"It's just a little—a little sudden." She chuckled weakly. "What a damnable missish thing to say!"

"I've been home for six weeks, Renna, and every moment I've been learning about you from your cousin, from my mother—Good God, do you think I propose to every female I meet?"

"If this weren't entirely out of your mother's style I would say that she had concocted the whole thing out of piece cloth. She has been determined to marry me off since I arrived, and pressing me to make a match for you and—I know not with whom."

"Mamma is wiser than she seems sometimes. Won't you even consider it, Renna? Can't I appeal even to the sense in you? Do you truly wish for nothing more than a future as a maiden-aunt–companion? If you do—but you can't. If you will consider my suit for no other reason—"

"Do you think you are being kindly to a lost soul doomed to unhappy maidenhood? I beg to inform you that I do very well as I am, and have no need to be protected from a life of genteel poverty!" she said hotly, then realized that Lyn might well be completely unaware of her wealth. No matter, she thought. I can tell him later. If there is a later.

"Damn. I make it worse and worse. Renna, believe me: I don't mean to make such a mull of this. I've never asked anyone to marry me before. And I don't expect to do so again. I admit I'm not very polished at it, but I'd not meant to make such a horse's—"

It was too much; she began to chuckle. "Spare my blushes, please! I don't mean to be so difficult, Lyn. It's just that—" Her voice dropped rather unsteadily. "It's just that, of all the things I have wanted to hear in the last few weeks, this is the one I thought I never would."

He took a step closer. "If it will convince you that I am perfectly and entirely serious, Rowena my very dear love, I shall be more graceless still." And without giving her time to reply he pulled her away from the bookcase and into his arms, looking down from his surprising height at her confusion.

After a moment Rowena managed, with a very notable attempt at composure, "I suppose you had better kiss me, Lyn, for if you do not I shall kiss you, and complete the destruction of my reputation entirely."

So he bent his head: just a little way, as she was taller than he had thought. It was a tentative, smiling sort of kiss. The second one was something more, breathless and fiery, and both of them were blushing and a little startled when it was through.

Five minutes later, seated together on the sofa, they began to talk rationally again.

"I shall have to give this ribbon up entirely." She teased him. "Look, you have completely torn it out of my hair. Are you always such a savage, love?"

"Only in the midst of proposing, sweetheart. Hereafter I shall be as meek as a lamb."

"And bore me dreadfully, doubtless. Well, I

seem to have fulfilled my Aunt Dorothea's predictions and become entirely mad. Madness is pleasanter than I would have thought."

"A consummation devoutly to be wished, in fact," he agreed. "But I'm still waiting for my answer. You will marry me, won't you?"

"I had best, I suppose. Even on the continent I should never be allowed in anyone's drawing room unmarried after that kiss. Caro Lamb is nothing to it."

"Thank God for the conventions!" Mr. Bradwell breathed devoutly, and kissed the tip of her ear.

"But Lyn?" She looked at him seriously, the smallest of smiles waiting in the corner of her mouth. "Do you think we should perhaps wait until tomorrow to announce *our* engagement?"

"I suppose so; after all, Jane and Jack have precedence," he agreed judiciously. Another long, sweet kiss. "But by the day after tomorrow we had best be formally betrothed or I shall not answer for your reputation or mine."

"Very well, Mr. Bradwell, on the day after tomorrow *we* shall be the happy couple. That is, of course, providing that your mamma and Dr. Cribbatt do not surprise us after all."

Chapter 9

Lady Bradwell proved unable to affiance herself to the doctor, or to anyone else, before dinnertime, and afterward, when the party was gathered in the drawing room, Lord Bradwell pleased the company (with the possible exception of his sister-at-law-to-be) by announcing his engagement to Jane Ambercot. Ulysses, who had arrived early in the afternoon to visit with Margaret, was applied to in his capacity as head of the Ambercot household, and his consent was readily and publicly supplied, with a few exhortations not to be such an abominably slowmoving couple when they were wedded. Lord

Bradwell tried, with an effort quite visible on his beaming countenance, to produce a suitably tart reply, but in the end only laughed and thanked his new brother.

"I say, Miss Rowena, if Ambercot's marrying your cousin and I'm marrying Janie, that relates you to our family, don't it?"

Rowena sternly ignored the secret, sharing smile from Lyn and answered noncommittally that she supposed that it did.

"Indeed, and it means that Mr. Lyndon will be related to our family as well," Eliza said sweetly. "Ought I to call you cousin, sir?"

"I think..." Lady Bradwell answered for her son with the barest touch of frost in her voice, "that Lyn will do very well for now, child. Have you not always called him so? Or some variation on that? Well, I am ready to drink to our happy couples! May all you children be blessed with happiness, virtue, and more children for me to amuse myself over." The old lady raised her glass of ratafia solemnly and drained it. "Now, I think I have had a little more excitement than Dr. Cribbatt and his excellent assistant would prescribe. I plan to retire before tea." Totally unaware of the looks exchanged by several members of the company, she raised herself from her chair. "Renna, my dear, can I trouble you to assist me to my room?"

"Certainly, but I shall trouble you not to talk nonsense. There is no trouble to it." Exchanging a smile she thought unseen with Lyn, Rowena draped a shawl across Lady Bradwell's shoulders and offered her arm.

"Good night, my dears," Lady Bradwell called from the doorway, and was answered in a disorganized chorus of good nights and sleep wells.

Once out of the room, however, Lady Bradwell appeared to recover a good deal of her strength. "We have pulled it off—even Jack and Jane, dear foolish children that they are, *cannot* announce their engagement and cry off again twice in one lifetime! I begin to see hope. Now if only—"

"You can marry Mr. Bradwell off, you will be perfectly happy," Rowena finished for her.

Lady Bradwell regarded her with a speculative eye. "Well, of course, child. Then it would only be to wait for the first grandchildren. I find I am becoming dreadfully dynastic in my old age. Are you sure I cannot persuade you to take on Lyn's case, Renna?"

"As matchmaker? Now, really ma'am," Rowena began, privately a little ashamed of her resolution to keep her secret even one night.

Lady Bradwell continued her scrutiny. "You know very well what I mean, girl. I've a notion, what's more, that you don't altogether dislike the idea of Lyn."

"Surely it's more to the point wether he dislikes the idea of *me*, Lady B."

"Either my eyes are better than you give me credit for, my dear, or yours are very bad indeed. Well, I shan't meddle—not just now, in any case. When you, or Lyn, or both of you come to your senses, I shall be waiting to hear about it."

"Ma'am." Rowena's voice was serious now. "What makes you think that we should suit?"

"Child, what makes *you* think that any two people should suit? You're both bright, handsome people with a little more than the common share of sense and ambition, and thankfully, each of you knows when to laugh. For God's sake, Rowena, even if I'm wrong about you and my boy—although I misdoubt that I am; it seems perfectly obvious to me—don't settle for someone who doesn't share your sense of humor. It's all very well for Jack and Jane to wed, for neither one of them looks at things the way you do, or I, or Lyn; but did you marry someone like Jack you'd be bored and fractious within a month. Now, you know I'm rather partial to my Lyn—don't smirk at me, you odious chit—but I do think that you two *would* suit. And it would make me very happy."

"Well, ma'am." They had reached Lady Bradwell's room and Rowena was about to ring for the maid to come and attend her mistress. "Whatever happens, I thank you for loving me well enough to want me for your favorite son. And just now, I shall thank you more particularly for going to sleep. You *are* looking a little gray and weary, and whatever your son's opinion of me, it will not redound to my credit if I permit you to fall sick again."

Rowena left her mistress in Taylor's admirable hands and descended to the saloon again only to find that the men had retired to the library to drink a few healths to the ladies and each other. Jane, Eliza, and Margaret sat quietly talking in the parlor and after a time, when the congratulatory noise from the library grew stronger, Rowena suggested that Eliza spend the night, and that all of them retire in short order. It was an anticlimax after the celebration of dinner, and Rowena had privately hoped for a minute alone with Lyn before she slept. Nonetheless she summoned Mrs. Coffee and had a room prepared for Eliza, seeing to the girl's comfort before taking herself to her own room.

On the dressing table was a note, inscribed in a small, precise hand. "Breakfast? I love you. Lyn." Smiling, Rowena undressed, washed, and slipped into bed, where she fell asleep quickly to dream of Lyn and warm days of happiness.

After a very good night's sleep Rowena woke before the maid arrived to kindle the fire. She lay in bed luxuriously for half an hour, watching sunlight establish itself in the room, and chatted cheerfully with the girl when she entered with a kettle of hot water and the tinderbox.

"What time is breakfast laid out, Kitty?"

"Abaht half-seven, miss, though nawone's theer at table afore nine, mawstly."

"Well, I think I shall go down early this morning. Is it as fair out as it looks from my window?"

"'Tis a fine, fair day, miss. Wi' you need me annymahr?"

Rowena, examining the fine, fair day for herself from the window, dismissed the maid and, after reading Lyn's brief note two or three times and scolding herself for romantic foolishness, began to wash.

It was not quite eight when she arrived in the breakfast room; Lyn was already there, being served coffee by Drummey. He rose, greeted her, and when the butler had retired to fetch hot water for tea, crossed the room to kiss her.

"If you promise to kiss me every morning before tea I think I shall like being married very much. It improves this hour immeasurably."

"You got my note?" he asked from a vantage point just above her right ear, where the breath from each word tickled her distractingly.

"Of course. It's a wonder it isn't torn and tattered by now. It's such a short, sweet little thing I have read it fifty times already this morning."

"Next time I'll write something a little longer and meatier, darling. I'm sorry I didn't see you after you took Mamma up last night, but..."

"I shall have to accustom myself to being abandoned for your jollifications with the men," Rowena answered in tones of deep martyrdom. "After all, a woman's place—"

"Good God, Rowena, I beg you not to start! If you're going to lecture me a platform on the martyrdom of females—I shan't believe you at all. You're not the sort of woman who would lend herself to being ill used in any case. And you're much too beautiful for me to *want* to leave you solely to look at my brother's face or your friend Ambercot's! On the other hand,"

—he smiled at her—"I did feel rather celebratory last evening. Do you blame me?"

Rowena gave up the expression of dignified resignation she had assumed with a chuckle. "Not in the least. I felt so myself, and believe me, Lyn, it was very hard to keep from telling your mamma what was afoot when she pressed me to make a match for you."

"Well, love, today we can tell her you have complied with her wishes. On all counts." He pressed a kiss on the nape of her neck. "What did Mamma say?"

"Nothing terribly important. Only, she does love you, Lyn, and I think she will not be unhappy when we give her our news."

A light kindled in his eye: "Why don't we go awaken the old girl, wish her joy, and give her our news right now."

"Because," Miss Cherwood answered crisply, smoothing the somewhat disturbed folds of his neckcloth, "your mamma needs her sleep, and *I* need my tea, and Drummey will be back here in a moment, and I should like to be kissed once more before I resume the mask of propriety."

Lyn complied not once but several times, holding her very closely and murmuring appropriate comments between kisses. Only a tactful rattle at the door latch gave them any warning that Drummey was about to enter with the tea water, and when he entered he found Mr. Bradwell in the process of seating Miss Cherwood at table.

"I wonder how much Drummey knows, or suspects, of us?" Lyn said wryly when the butler was gone again.

"Considerably more than you'd think, I reckon. We had a maid in Vienna who I could have sworn was a mind reader, and Drummey strikes me as another such. Clara and Mamma would have fiercesome discussions, neither understanding the other, since Clara spoke no English and Mama not a word of German. But when something was to be done, or the time when we were harboring a fellow from the authorities—Lord, that was a story, Lyn! Clara was the only one of the staff who knew, although no one had told her. And very properly did she act, when pressed to it, too."

"Will you be content to settle yourself with a poor politician after all your adventures, sweetheart?"

"When it has always been my ambition to run a salon with my hair in Recamier ringlets and lounge upon a sofa being witty and charming? Why, I'd marry you for the chance of that even if you were bandy-legged and cross-eyed and spoke with a stutter."

"If those are your requirements..." He helped her to a slice of beef. "I shall try to bandy my legs and cross my eyes. The stutter will take a little more work, but I'm certain I can acquire one in due course. Seriously, Renna, you know it will be some time before there can be any questions of a salon."

"Well of course, I should dislike to appear to

be a mushroom or a cit. If you say the salon must wait then wait it shall."

"Several things will have to wait until I can establish myself, love. I have sent out letters to Castlereagh and Sidmouth, and I'm hoping to hear something good from them, with Uncle Kelvin's support. But for a while I shan't be able to do more than feed you and clothe you." She looked at him in dismay. "No, not quite that bad, my dear, but as a second son, you know...Well, if we do marry soon, and I hope we shall marry *very* soon"—his look warmed her— "we shall simply have to be a little careful, is all."

"I'm used to that, Lyn. I cannot begin to tell you what a luxury it is to live in a place where I needn't constantly translate for myself, or worry because the messenger with funds for Mamma or Papa has disappeared and we're down to the last pullet in the yard, or because soldiers—any soldiers at all, English, French, Spanish, German, whatever!—have been sighted a few miles from the house and all the maids have run to hide themselves under the beds crying *'Aiii, Santa Maria ayúdame!'* I don't mind being careful, as you call it."

"I just don't want you to form one idea of what our life will have to be at first and then—" he began, deliberately ignoring her teasing.

"Well," she interrupted diplomatically. "I do have a little money of my own."

"Do you think I'd touch whatever independence you have? That will be tied up properly for you and the children." He flushed slightly. "I shall see to that."

Rowena returned his look warmly, but continued. "But Lyn, love, we could tie up a great deal for the children and myself and still live comfortably—not elegantly, but comfortably—on what is left, at least until you catch the eye of someone in the government."

"What do you mean?"

"Well, certainly I don't think you would want to run for a seat from my pocket, and I doubt I should care for it either. But—"

"Rowena, just what do you mean by a little money?" Lyn asked quietly. She looked at him in suprise, a little guiltily.

"Your mamma hasn't talked to you? No, I suppose she wouldn't. I was funning you a little, Lyn. My parents left me some money is all. You had no idea?"

"I know nothing of how your parents left you. I had assumed that you were—forgive me, but—quite impoverished. Else why would you be here working for my mother?"

"Because, given the choice of living respectably and properly and boringly with my aunt, taking part in the innumerable skirmishes that seem to develop between her and me, and hiring myself out as a companion to someone who really needed me, there *was* no choice. I'm not eccentric enough to set myself up in an establishment with hired chaperones, and I couldn't live with my aunt any longer. I've been a grown woman, responsible for the management of my life and an establishment for too long to be reduced comfortably to unmarried-niece status and married off to the first convenient peer who offered for me. That was what I faced at Aunt Doro's, Lyn. Do you wonder that I chose as I did? Your mamma knows the whole of the story, and didn't object to the fact that I have an easy competence—well, perhaps a little better than that."

"Just how much better?" he asked sternly.

"Lyn?" She looked at him, uneasy at the tone in his voice.

"Rowena, just how easy a competence is it? I have a right to know, don't I?"

She steeled herself to meet his gaze. Suddenly everything felt wrong, strained. But she owed him an honest answer. "There's forty thousand invested in the Navy Fives, and another—I don't know, perhaps twelve hundred a year from the revenues at Styles—that was Papa's estate—and the rent of the house and grounds, too, since we haven't lived there in above seven years. A little less than four thousand a year, I suppose." She tried to say it nonchalantly.

Lyn had put his fork and knife down and was studying his coffee cup with interest. "You couldn't have told me all this before, I suppose?"

"Good God, Lyndon Bradwell, what was I supposed to do? Inform you, when you stumbled upon me at the duck pond that afternoon, that I was worth four thousand a year to the lucky man who could snag me? Lord, I can see it now: 'Good Afternoon, sir. Bradwell, d'you say? How d'you do? I'm Rowena Cherwood, heiress, companion to your mamma.' Would it have made that much of a difference?"

"To my loving you? No." Her heart skipped a beat and she looked up, but his face was still closed and remote. "To my speaking of it—I don't know. It ought to. Rowena, suddenly you're Cophetua and I the beggar. It won't—damn it, it won't fadge. I can't set myself up on your money, and it don't seem fair to drag you along in careful poverty until I've found my place."

"Even if I wish to be dragged? Lyn, what are you saying? Don't I get a say in the matter?"

"Of course you do. But suddenly—I'm not sure if I should do this to either of us, Renna. No more than I think I can stand to let you go. Suppose you were to wake up one morning and realize that you resented me for marrying you and living off your money?"

"Then hang the money!" she cried impatiently. "For heaven's sake, Lyn."

"All right, suppose we do 'hang the money' as you say. Then, what if you wake one morning to realize that you might have had your salon and Recamier ringlets and a place in society by marrying differently?"

"O, Lyn." She pursed her lips together, trying to rally arguments. "What doth it profit me if I gain my ringlets and lose *you?* You wouldn't—after all this muddlesome business, you wouldn't jilt me because I'm an heiress, would you?"

He only looked uncomfortable.

"Lyn, for heaven's sake, I'll give my money to the first beggar I meet, and follow you barefoot if need be." She stared at him, unable to believe the stranger he had become in minutes. "Before God, love, I never thought I'd think my money a curse! It's been inconvenient sometimes, but now I thought that it would be a godsend to us. Instead—"

He broke in bitterly. "Did you think that you could set yourself up in your salon, and me in a pocket borough? We'd be grand acquisitions for the party, wouldn't we, love. Bradwell and his wealthy wife."

"Lyndon Bradwell," Rowena said quietly. "You would have married me practically from the gutter and made me the wife of a rising politico—" He made a motion to deny her theatrical words. "No, damn it, if you intend to sound like a Covent Garden melodrama I shall certainly oblige you with all the fustian I can muster. *You* can bring what you will to this marriage, but *I* cannot? And you will let your stupid male pride get in the way of—" Her voice broke.

"Rowena!"

She regained her control. "Don't say anything. I'm not finished yet. I have practically thrown myself at you this morning, not once but twice. Three is reported to be the charm. Do you want *me*, Lyn, and do you want me enough to disregard my fortune, or my lack of fortune, or your lack of fortune, or whatever? You've said we would not starve if I married you—which is all I ask. I can consign my money to the devil happily if need be. But if you cannot accept that, I will not trouble to humble myself further."

"Rowena? God, don't you understand what I'm afraid of? If I were to come to feel that I'd taken advantage of you—I couldn't—damn it, I don't know what to tell you."

"Remains only for me to act then," she said with a lightness she was far from feeling. The tea in her cup was cold and very bitter. "I'm sorry, Lyn. I could have married you and forgotten about the tiresome money entirely. I was quite serious. I'd have lived in a cottage, on broth and bread for the rest of my days, if you'd offered them to me. That's how foolish I am. But if you cannot do the same, forget that I mentioned it. Forget I—forget I ever came down to breakfast with you. I could have married you with or without the money, but I will not marry you against your will, and certainly not if you're afraid to become some sort of villain by it."

She rose from the table and walked deliberately from the room.

For a moment Bradwell simply sat, watching, unable to believe what he and she and they together had done. Then, "Rowena!" He sprang from his chair and went to peer out into the hallway. She had vanished. He returned to the table to sit among the wreckage of his forgotten breakfast, head in hands, damning himself for every kind of fool imaginable.

Rowena had not retired to her room to be haunted there by the sight of that brief note—

his first and last love letter to her—and her dreams of the night before. Instead, she went into the office and made herself ferociously busy with accounts and inventories. When she heard the door to the breakfast room open and close, and the sound of boot heels vanishing toward the courtyard door, she breathed a little easier and relaxed her grip on the pen between her fingers, feeling the blood flow again. She was too angry to cry, too shattered to do anything but play at toting up rows of figures. In a flash of humor she thought wryly, I shall have to re-do all this work tomorrow in any case. But the thought of tomorrow was unpleasant enough to be relegated to the same blackness as the thought of Lyn and the scant day of happiness they had shared together.

After a while—perhaps an hour or more, although Rowena's sense of time had seemingly deserted her entirely—there was a timid knock on the door and Drummey appeared.

"I beg your pardon, Miss Cherwood, but there is a woman—a lady at the door, who says that she is *Mrs.* Cherwood." His tone bespoke utter bafflement, and his slight stress on the word *lady* said worlds for Drummey's opinion of the visitor, whatever her birth.

"Mrs. Cherwood? O no, it couldn't be!" Rowena collected herself. "Thank you, Drummey. I shall join her directly in the green saloon. And will you send to see if Miss Margaret has arisen yet?"

"I had taken the liberty to do so, miss," he

assured her, his tone implying a sympathy he could not openly offer.

"Thank you, then." Rowena stood to collect herself. In her own mind she imagined she looked a harridan, but the mirror returned the image of a tall, handsome woman, quietly but elegantly dressed in green sarsanet, her dark hair in an informal classical knot atop her head. Her expression was sober, but only her eyes betrayed her inner turmoil and shock. "I shall have to do," she admonished her reflection, and left for the green saloon.

A woman was waiting for her there, examining a Chinese vase and, by the look of her, appraising it for every sixpence of its worth. She was short, stocky, with grizzled hair under an elaborate poke-bonnet, and a ruddy complexion fought unsuccessfully with her puce traveling gown. Even that garment's exquisite tailoring could not hide the defects of a stubby figure and short neck, and Rowena, taking in the sight of the lady, spared a moment to be thankful for Ulysses Ambercot's sake that Margaret resembled the Cherwoods rather than her mother's family.

"Good morning, Aunt Dorothea," she said quietly. The woman turned.

"Rowena, my dear!" she said in enthusiastic accents. "But how very poorly you look!"

Chapter 10

The welcome accorded Mrs. Dorothea Cherwood on her arrival at Broak could best be described as cordially distasteful. Lady Bradwell and her sons, as well as Anne Ambercot and her children, had heard enough of the new arrival's past antics to be guarded, at least, in their welcoming. Margaret, for all she tried to act the dutiful daughter, was stopped from slipping quietly into the role by Ulysses, who took matters in hand with a tact Rowena would have thought above his touch, and made it clear to Mrs. Cherwood with words unspoken that her daughter was now *his* fiancée, and not to be ill used, even by her mother. After a quick appraisal of a situation which necessitated her arising earlier than she had in years, Lady Bradwell decided that it was safe at least to leave Meggy to Lully's devoted care. It was Rowena for whom the lady was truly concerned.

Miss Cherwood, busy directing Mrs. Coffee to establish Mrs. Cherwood in one of the guest rooms and to make sure her maid and grooms were billeted comfortably, assumed for the first time in her months at Broak the mien and carriage of a servant. Lady Bradwell, unaware of the passages between her son and her companion, assumed that the girl's sudden depression was entirely due to her aunt's appearance, and took an even firmer dislike to the unpopular Mrs. Cherwood. In fact, the only person in the house who seemed to rub along at all well with Margaret's mother was Lully's sister Eliza. "Which, when you come to think of it, makes a dreadful sort of sense," Lady Bradwell confided to her favorite son. "Dearly as I love Margaret, I cannot help but wonder how long we are to be favored with her mother's presence."

Lyn also had a distracted air, and it took him a moment to recall what the subject of the conversation was. "O, yes. Odious woman. It's luck for Miss Margaret that Ambercot seems determined to stand up for her. Did you see their meeting, Mamma?"

Lady Bradwell had not been one of the witnesses to Mrs. Cherwood's reunion with her youngest daughter, but she had heard all about it. Dorothea Cherwood, unable to wait until the girl could be roused from her bed, dressed, and brought down to the saloon where refreshments had been laid, swept past her niece, up the stairs, trumpeting Margaret's name. Meg's maid said later that the girl had risen from a sound sleep with a look of confusion and distress, just in time to be swept to her maternal bosom while Mrs. Cherwood made a romantic and almost unintelligible speech about the strength of a Mother's Love.

The household, from scullery to parlor, was displeased by Mrs. Dorothea Cherwood; that day was a very long one.

It seemed doubly long to Rowena, earnestly pursuing as many tasks as she could decently find for herself, and to Lyn, who had taken himself out to waste good shot in firing at pigeons and crows in the long meadow. Lady Bradwell had descended to greet her unlooked-for guest and, after appraising the situation, deemed it advisable to stay below and guard her nest, sending for reinforcement in the shape of Anne Ambercot. Had Mrs. Cherwood been aware of the stir she was causing at Broak she would have been highly gratified.

When the party convened at dinner Mrs. Cherwood made herself the focus of attention, or rather, finding herself the focus, made the most of her position. She lectured Jane Ambercot on the proper upkeep of a young lady's hands, recommending frequent applications of lemon juice followed by Denmark Lotion to remove freckles and preserve a soft and genteel appearance. She suggested to Mrs. Ambercot, with the privilege of one soon to be related, that perhaps her turban was a trifle outré, even for the depths of rural Devonshire. She made recommendations in the most confiding manner to Lady Bradwell on a very clever fellow in Eastcheap who did reweaving, for that little patch of fraying carpet on the third-floor stairway, and advised her to air all her tapestries with lavender and comfrey. She made coy remarks to Lord Bradwell and Mr. Ambercot about their nearing nuptial bliss, and advised Mr. Lyndon Bradwell to take his brother's lead and follow suit. When Mr. Bradwell scowled at this, she suggested salts or hartshorn, or a tisane of chamomile and wintergreen for the headache he appeared to have. And throughout the meal, indeed throughout the evening, she found fault with Rowena.

She looked positively hagged. Well, Mrs. Cherwood had always thought that Renna's beauty wasn't of the lasting sort, and see, the girl had turned down a very advantageous offer which was likely to be the best she would ever get. She would surely never get another if she continued to deteriorate in this fashion, poor thing. Did Renna advise Lady Bradwell on the doings of the servants' hall? Mrs. Cherwood hoped that Lady Bradwell had her own spies in the kitchen, then, for while Rowena was a dear girl, she had been brought up so much abroad, you know, that she really could have no idea of how things were done in a proper English house. Mrs. Cherwood expressed great surprise that Lady Bradwell permitted Rowena the management of the house accounts and tenantry books; surely such things were better left to a factor or steward. A young female could never really understand such complex matters.

By the time dinner had ended and the ladies, withdrawn to the drawing room, found themselves stranded with Margaret's mother, she had alienated everyone in the house except for Eliza Ambercot. The two of them sat, an issue of the *Ladies' Companion* open between them, and talked of gowns, hair pomade, and gossip.

If she thought about it at all, Rowena was rather more grateful than not for her aunt's arrival, as it gave her something to think of beyond her own misery. She was not up to retaliating for the slights heaped upon her, but now and then the absurdity of the situation dawned on her, asserting itself in a faint, self-mocking smile. Mrs. Cherwood never saw the smile, and believed smugly that a life in service was humbling her intractable niece.

Lyn, stationed across the room from Rowena and Margaret, would have liked very much to offer the elder Miss Cherwood the same sort of protection that Ulysses Ambercot had extended to his betrothed. Indeed, shortly before dinner he had met Rowena en route to her room, and asked, or rather tried to ask, if there was anything he could do to help her.

"With what, Mr. Bradwell?" Miss Cherwood asked dully.

"Rowena, look." She did not. "Confound it, Renna, I'm every kind of fool if you like, although I still maintain—"

"I really don't wish to listen to this, Lyn," she said wearily. "If you meant to ask if you could help with my aunt, I don't see how. If you pay her too much attention it will make her worse than with none at all. I can handle her. At least Meggy don't have to go back there for any length of time. Aunt Doro is so thrilled at marrying off her last daughter that she's practically ready to marry Meg from your dining room. For your mother's sake I would advise you to discourage her in that notion as soon as possible." Dropping something close to a housemaid's bob, Rowena escaped him. They had not spoken since.

The evening was, if possible, longer than the long day had been. Mrs. Cherwood protested herself charmed with everything, joined in a game of whist, advised, uninvited, upon a game of backgammon, and boisterously queried Margaret from across the room as to what she was doing. When, shortly before ten, Rowena gathered up her tambour work and needle and very firmly suggested to Lady Bradwell that it was time she made her farewells and retired, Mrs. Cherwood said good night to her hostess in forthright fashion, her sharp eye missing nothing of Rowena's solicitous care for her mistress.

"My dear, do come in and sit awhile," Lady Bradwell entreated when they reached her room. "I don't think you need return downstairs again, unless you really wish to do."

Rowena smiled faintly. "Am I that obvious, ma'am? Your wish is my command, of course." She sat heavily on a chair near the bed and rang for Taylor.

"Thank God Margaret takes after your side of the family, my love. What a fright of a woman! Although I should not say so to you."

"My dear Lady B, when I have been filling you full of the most outrageous calumnies against my good aunt for all these months! You needn't scruple to tell me if you merely agree with me." Almost, Rowena had regained her own old tone. But not quite.

"My dear, is it only your dreadful aunt's arrival that has you so knocked up?" Lady Bradwell asked solicitously. "I suppose I ought not to ask that either, but I dislike to see you so mopey. What's blue-deviled you? Yesterday you seemed full of smiles, or was that only for Jack and Jane?"

"Yesterday I *was* full of smiles," Rowena agreed. "Today I'm not so. I suspect I am only tired, ma'am. And Aunt Doro's presence here is something of a strain." Miss Cherwood bent her head to examine a cross-stitch on her embroidery.

"And on Lyn as well?" Lady Bradwell asked shrewdly. Rowena's head snapped up. "O, come child, credit me with a little intelligence! I can see *something,* after all. What has that wretched boy done to hurt you? Or, is it you has hurt him?" The older woman's tone was level; there was no sound of recrimination in her voice, certainly nothing to send Miss Cherwood into a fit of tears. But in a moment the companion had dissolved into sobs, struggling to breathe as much as to stifle the unexpected outpouring of her misery. When she was a little more in command of herself Rowena realized that she had been seated on the bed next to her mistress, and had been crying very noisily onto that lady's shoulder, soaking through a Norwich shawl and the fichu of her evening dress.

"I d-d-do beg your pardon, ma'am," she gasped at last. "I don't normally make a cake of myself in this fashion."

"Since you have never done so before I am inclined to believe you," Lady Bradwell replied drily. "Don't be such a peahen, child. I shan't melt under a few tears. Now, are you going to be a good girl and tell me what sort of May game you and Lyn are playing at? He hasn't—"

"What?" Rowena asked damply.

"He hasn't asked you—no, he wouldn't do such a thing. He's not so lost to the proprieties, even if he is sometimes a clodpole. If he's been a trifle maladroit, my love, you should remember that he hasn't been home in so long he's probably forgotten how to treat a civilized woman."

"My dearest Lady B, you don't imagine that

176

Mr. Bradwell offered me a carte blanche, do you?" Shakily at first, then more heartily, Rowena began to laugh. Lady Bradwell regarded her companion with something like alarm. "O, O dear! No, ma'am, I am sorry. I assure you I'm not run mad." Rowena began to compose herself. "I ought not to laugh at it," she said at last. "In fact, Mr. Bradwell's scruples border on the exquisite! So far from offering me a straw marriage, he has withdrawn an offer of real marriage so that he can not be accused of marrying me for my fortune!"

Louisa Bradwell gaped at the younger woman.

"No son of mine," she said at last, "could say anything so fustian!"

"I am devastated to correct you, ma'am, but a son of yours has done so. If you please, I am Cophetua and he the beggar maid. Or man, rather. He won't have it bruited about that he married me for my money. Granted, I'm far from being a pauper, but if he had asked it I would have consigned the money to the devil; at least, I think I should have done, although it seems like a stupid thing to do. Do men always expect these absurd sacrifices of one?"

"But couldn't you talk him out of the notion, Renna?" Lady Bradwell asked pleadingly. She had woven a daydream about her companion and her younger son, and the children seemed determined to destroy it for her.

"I assure you, I tried, ma'am. I tried to joke him out of it; then I tried to argue the notion from him. No help for it: He is determined that both of us shall be miserable. Perhaps it is better that you find someone else for my position, ma'am." Miss Cherwood's voice quavered on the edge of tears again.

"If that is what you truly wish, I shall make arrangements," Lady Bradwell said astringently, in a voice that barred tears. "But I dislike to think of you returning to live with that dreadful woman again."

"Aunt Doro? Perish the thought, ma'am. If you can give me a good letter of reference, I surely can find another position in a short while. And perhaps Aunt Anne and Lully and Jane can put up with me for a time until I do."

"I still think it the foolishest thing I have ever heard of. Rowena, *do* you love Lyn?"

"At the moment," Miss Cherwood assured her employer evenly, "I could watch him being drawn and quartered. And applaud."

"Of course you could." Lady Bradwell was sympathetic. "But do you love him?"

Rowena sighed heavily. "Yes, I love him. God knows why, for he's the stupidest, proudest, most unreachable—drat him, I do love him. I think I must be completely insane."

"And he loves you," Lady Bradwell stated, as if trying to solve a difficult puzzle.

"He said so," Rowena returned dully. "That was the excuse he gave for breaking off our silly little understanding."

"Well, then." Lady Bradwell sighed contentedly. "I think we should be able to contrive reasonably well. Don't be in too great a hurry to pack up your bags, child. You may drop a few hints, if you wish. No, better. Ask Anne Ambercot if you may come and stay with her for a short while in the near future. Surely that will get back to Lyn and—"

"Machinations, Lady B? I don't want Lyn by tricks."

"Not tricks, dear. But sometimes one does have to stimulate a man's thought processes by dealing him a shock. Let me talk to Lyn. I vow I shall not let him know what you have told me. I should rather like to hear my own son convict himself of pomposity and stupidity from his own mouth. Now, girl, it is time you were in bed."

Indeed, Rowena was exhausted. For the first time since her arrival at Broak months before, it was Miss Cherwood who was taken to her room by her mistress and ordered to sleep.

With Rowena gone from the drawing room a slight edge of Mrs. Cherwood's triumph was gone, and she became a little less strident. Only a little less. Lyn, Lord Bradwell, and Ulysses Ambercot had withdrawn from the room, and Jane and Margaret deliberately set themselves up in a conversation on neighborhood charity that was so unexceptionable that Mrs. Cherwood could not object, and so uninteresting that Eliza had no inclination to join in. The two outcasts of the party, completely unaware of their ostracism, continued together, talking of bonnets, town scandal, and finally, deliciously, of the romances at Broak.

"Of course I shall be delighted to have Dearest Margaret for my sister," Eliza gushed. "Lully is simply ears over heels in love with her."

"Such an affecting sight," Mrs. Cherwood agreed sentimentally. "And your sister and Lord Bradwell make a—a striking couple, do not they?"

"O yes, although I have never much cared for Janie's sort of looks. But Lord Bradwell does well enough, particularly in evening dress. What a shame he can talk of nothing but shooting and horses!"

"But what of you, my dear?" Mrs. Cherwood asked archly. "Haven't you a young suitor hidden about?" She made a show of looking around the room, to be rewarded only by the sight of Margaret and Jane deep in conversation, and Mrs. Ambercot nodding slightly over her writing case. She rapped Eliza's knuckles coyly, painfully, with her fan. "Ah, you young things! I'll wager there are a half-dozen beaux quite mad for you!"

Eliza blushed, looked gratified. "Well, one or two, ma'am," she managed to say modestly. "But they're all such *boys*. And since I've returned from Tunbridge I find I simply have no patience with boys." She assumed a tone becoming a forty-year-old matron in its weary sophistication. Mrs. Cherwood seemed to find nothing amiss in being so addressed by a chit of eighteen, however.

"How true. Ah, my dear Miss Eliza, is there

no one?" On an inspiration she turned to regard the door through which the gentlemen had vanished some fifteen minutes before. "Perhaps a neighbor? Soon to be related by marriage, perhaps?" Mrs. Cherwood was rewarded for this piece of guessing by a conscious blush from Eliza. "Well, then, my dear, surely that man is lost! Such a pretty thing as you are—" With Margaret settled, there was no reason not to be generous, Dorothea Cherwood reasoned. "So I see that this house party really *is* complete! Three couples, three marriages. Why, I declare it is like something on the stage."

"But Miss Cherwood, that is, Miss Rowena Cherwood, doesn't have—I mean..." Eliza faltered, afraid to say too much to someone who was, after all, Rowena's aunt.

"O, Rowena," Mrs. Cherwood scoffed. "She's past her prayers, that one. Completely her fault, too, since I had lined up the most advantageous match for her! What must she do but go and hire herself out as a servant. Not that the Bradwells are not everything that is genteel and agreeable, of course." Her tone made Rowena's degradation entirely her own fault.

"Of course." Eliza smiled, sensing a comrade.

"Sorry as I feel for Rowena, I have very little patience with her. She wanted to go into service, and that is the life she has made for herself. After all, what sort of man will want her now? And she is no longer young, although I will admit that she has kept her looks for a remarkably long time."

Eliza had an inspiration so breathtaking she was almost afraid to voice it. Could she enlist Mrs. Cherwood—Margaret's mother, Rowena's aunt, what could be more appropriate!—in her plans for Lyndon Bradwell's attachment? It required, first of all, that Rowena Cherwood be settled elsewhere, and short of taking the veil, marriage was the most permanent disposition for a young woman of which Miss Ambercot knew. "There is one man..." she murmured at last.

Mrs. Cherwood looked into her companion's face. "A man, for Rowena?" Her tone was mingled displeasure and curiosity. After all, it would not necessarily be a bad thing to marry the girl off suitably. On the other hand, it rankled her to think of the girl marrying well after turning off Sir Jason Slyppe—Lord Slyppe, as he was now.

"Well, I do know one man who is very— very interested in Miss Rowena Cherwood. However, he has very meager funds at his command, and is not really what the world would term a great match, so that he has hesitated to speak to her." Eliza lied happily, certain that she had said something of interest. She was reasonably certain from Dorothea Cherwood's tone that helping Rowena to a marriage with a man like Greavesey would find approval from Mrs. Cherwood, and she watched the older woman's face for signs that her intuition was correct.

"Ah, well my dear," Mrs. Cherwood said at last, a sharkish smile hovering about her lips. "When a woman is no longer young or beautiful and has cast her better chances to the wind, she cannot hope for much choice. I do not believe that, after having been in service for nearly a year, Rowena would not prefer marriage—any marriage—to life as a companion, even to Lady Bradwell. Who is this man? I must certainly meet him."

"His name is Greavesey, ma'am. John Greavesey, I believe. He is the assistant to our doctor, Mr. Cribbatt."

A quick, delicious vision of Rowena huddled in a crowded cottage, brats hanging from her skirts, tired, worn with poverty and probably black-and-blue from a deserved beating by her husband, flashed through Mrs. Cherwood's mind. Then it was dispelled by her common sense. After all, Rowena had quite a good fortune. It was the reason why Sir Jason had been so eager to marry her, despite the fact that she towered over him by a good five inches. But perhaps this man, this Greavesey, was poor enough so that he would press Rowena into marriage and then do something dreadful and lowbred. Abandon her? Well, perhaps not. Again, Mrs. Cherwood relinquished an agreeable vision in which Rowena (and at least one very grubby infant) appealed to her aunt's charity, to be admitted as a dependent confined to the backstairs and nursery.

"I should very much like to meet this Mr. Greavesey." Mrs. Cherwood smiled again. Then, realizing that Meg and Jane, although still in conversation, had been casting looks in their direction: "As for you, my dear, persevere with your young man. You know these silly creatures. They never know what they want until a woman shows it to them. Margaret my love, you look altogether fagged. I think you had best retire. After all, we don't wish Dear Ulysses to think his bride-to-be is losing her looks, do we?"

Under her basilisk stare Margaret reluctantly rose and made her good nights to Mrs. Ambercot and her daughters. The party, or its remnants, abandoned the drawing room for the evening and retired to their respective rooms, with the exception of Mrs. Cherwood, who happily followed after her daughter to offer her a little advice, and to scold her again, most lovingly, for having run away to Broak and her cousin in the first place.

Despite her early retirement from the drawing room, it was observable the next morning that Miss Margaret was not in her best looks; her mother, on the other hand, looked as if she had slept like a top, and when Lyn Bradwell descended to breakfast well past his customary hour of nine, he found her following after Drummey, helpfully offering corrections to his technique with the polishing rag and suggesting a compound of lampblack and beeswax for silver tarnish. Sympathizing bleakly with the butler, Lyn withdrew to the breakfast room before Mrs. Cherwood could spot, and thus begin to make improvements on him, too.

Chapter 11

The excitements of the day before had proved
a little beyond Lady Bradwell's strength. In the
teeth of strong opposition she protested that she
was fit enough to descend to the saloon to sit up
there. Only the combined arguments of Rowena,
Margaret, and Mrs. Ambercot, together with a
solemn vow that the latter would stand in Lady
Bradwell's stead in the face of Mrs. Cherwood's
invasion, persuaded the older woman to rest.
Rowena, although she feared that it might be
Greavesey who responded rather than Dr. Cribbatt, sent a footman to the village to summon
the doctor just in case.

Had Mrs. Cherwood planned it, things could not have fallen out more agreeably.

Although neither Eliza Ambercot nor Dorothea Cherwood partook of breakfast, they found each other late that morning and settled comfortably in the garden room to chat and poke idly at their embroideries. Mrs. Cherwood lost very little time in reintroducing the subject of John Greavesey, and Eliza was happy to practice a little judicious misdirection by assuring Margaret's mother that Greavesey had long and silently pined for Rowena, and that Rowena might be persuaded to return his affection. Mrs. Cherwood was not much concerned with whether the feelings of either party were truly engaged; she was far too busy savoring the thought of her high and mighty niece, married to a doctor's assistant. The two ladies, under the sentimental guise of matchmaking, plotted happily over lemonade and biscuits on how to bring Greavesey to Broak for Mrs. Cherwood's inspection.

Before they could arrive at a suitable solution Eliza heard the voice of the man himself outside the door, and started up.

"Ma'am, I quite believe it is he!" Opening the door slightly, Eliza peered into the hallway, to be rewarded by the sight of Mr. Greavesey scuttling up the stairs like a cadaverous beetle.

"By all means then, child, desire one of the footmen to inform this Mr. Greavesey that I should like a word with him before he leaves," Mrs. Cherwood replied evenly. "And find me out where my niece is, will you?" Eliza, forgetting the dignity of eighteen in the delight of making mischief, set off as quickly as possible to reconnoiter.

Rowena was located in the herb garden, taking advantage of the fair weather to cut thyme and savory to dry in the kitchen. She wondered for a moment what Eliza Ambercot could be doing to make her trot about in such a fashion; her behavior was refreshingly unlike her normally affected prance. Rowena permitted herself the hope that perhaps Eliza was losing her affectations at last, and continued with her work.

There was something beneficial, after all, in cutting herbs; while it left a great deal of time for reflection, for replaying the last, horrible scene with Lyn over and over and over, still it allowed her some physical release. At some times the neat rows of parsley became Lyn, and she beheaded each one with relish. She was even able, for a time, to distract herself from the pressing urge to cry; she would come to it sooner or later, she assumed, but preferred to be in command of herself so long as Mrs. Cherwood remained in the house.

Ulysses Ambercot came upon her as she was finishing her chore, dusting off her hands and taking up the shears and basket.

"I say, Renna, that Greavesey is here again. Shall I send him about his business?"

Something like a martial light gleamed briefly in Rowena's eye: There, she thought, was a proper target for her wrath, not hapless parsley!

"No, Lully, I had ought to speak with him in any case. But I thank you for letting me know of him."

"Are you certain you don't want reinforcements? Meg would never forgive me if I turned tail and ran, to leave you to face the enemy."

"Lully, I beg your pardon, but I am *spoiling* for this," Rowena said with a cool glint in her eye. "If I vow that I shall not hit that odious man with one of the Chinese vases, nor throw the inkpot at him, nor do anything that is truly reprehensible, will you trust me?"

"Do I have another choice?" he asked wryly, and took the basket of greens from her. "At least let me bring these in to Cook, eh?"

"With pleasure. And Lully?" She touched his arm briefly. "You are a good man and a good friend. Margaret is a lucky woman." She smiled a smile of old friendship and disappeared into the house to wash her hands.

After examining Lady Bradwell, who made the matter rather difficult by taking him to task for his persecution of the females of her household, John Greavesey would have been very happy to have disappeared entirely from the face of the earth or, more particularly, from Broak, and was packing away his powders and jars when Drummey informed him that Mrs. Cherwood desired his company in the garden room.

At the name Cherwood, Greavesey winced.

He would have to face the music sometime or

other, but Rowena Cherwood did not appear to be the sort of woman to readily forgive him for importuning Jane Ambercot only because he had been thwarted elsewhere. It was with the severest misgivings that Mr. Greavesey allowed himself to be shown into the garden room. But the woman who waited there for him was not Rowena Cherwood. When she rose he noted that she was many years older, a head shorter than Miss Cherwood, and had a face not unlike an ill-favored dog.

"Ma'am?" he asked blankly.

"Mr. Greavesey?" The vision in purple sarsanet swept across the room to offer her hand to him. "I am delighted, utterly delighted! Permit me to introduce myself. I am Mrs. Cherwood. Dearest Margaret's mamma, you know."

Greavesey swallowed rapidly. He was unable to tell if Mrs. Cherwood had called him there to congratulate him on Margaret's recovery, or chastise him for his presumption in addressing her niece. While she continued effusively about the nobility of the medical profession he braced himself for a possible shock and tried to figure out this Mrs. Dorothea Cherwood.

"Now, sir," the lady was saying archly. "What's this a little bird has told me about you and that niece of mine?"

The devil, Greavesey thought. Here's for it.

But what came was not what he had expected. "I have heard hints, Mr. Greavesey, that you are not—ahh—impervious to my niece's charms, and she too..." She allowed herself to trail off suggestively. Recalling his last interview with Miss Cherwood, Greavesey found it a little difficult to follow Mrs. Cherwood's suggestion. "I wished you to know, Mr. Greavesey, that Rowena's uncle and I would not be averse to seeing her established with a good and honest man." That much Mrs. Cherwood could certainly say, for whatever her husband might say to the matter, she was sure he would not dislike to see his niece married. Whether he would like to see her married to this Greavesey was a different matter. For the rest, she thought, it would be as well that he *was* good, honest, virtuous, even conversable, for heaven knew that he was not likely to inspire passion in a maidenly breast on the basis of his looks. On consideration Mrs. Cherwood began to like the match better and better.

"Indeed, ma'am," Mr. Greavesey began rustily. "Indeed, ma'am, I have had—that is, I cherished certain—but Miss Cherwood seemed averse—that is, she seemed to dislike—although I thought—well, perhaps, ma'am—"

"Rowena," Mrs. Cherwood interrupted definately, "does not know what she wants. Why, my dear sir, it takes a man of decision to win a high-spirited girl such as my niece. And after all, there is her money as well as herself."

Greavesey looked up. "Her money, ma'am?"

"Why surely you know, Mr. Greavesey? Rowena has quite a nice little competence," Mrs. Cherwood understated happily. After all, she wanted to attract the man to Rowena, not scare him away completely, and Dorothea Cherwood doubted that this man would have the gumption to go after a woman with four thousand a year of her own. "Even if she is not as young or handsome as my Margaret, she does have her *dot,* and you must have seen how handily she manages here for Dear Lady Bradwell." Mrs. Cherwood's tone made Lady Bradwell one of her very closest friends.

"O, yes indeed Mrs. Cherwood." Greavesey gulped. "But do you think Miss Rowena would—I am, after all, a poor man, and when I last spoke to her—"

"My dear sir," she said airily. "No well-brought-up girl will tell her true feelings on the first application! It goes against everything that young girls are taught." She thought that that had got him.

"Why, ma'am, that was what I thought at the time. But Miss Cherwood seemed so particularly definite..." He trailed off doubtfully.

"Nonsense, sir. Rowena is a girl of spirit, that's all. Of course," Mrs. Cherwood continued, lest he disliked too much spirit in a woman, "it is only for some good man to take her in hand to have her meek as a lamb in jig time."

A golden vision of Rowena Cherwood—and her money—swam before John Greavesey's eyes. "If I spoke again, perhaps?"

"Certainly, Mr. Greavesey," Mrs. Cherwood encouraged. Now, all she had to do was speak with Rowena, make the girl understand that this was obviously to be her last chance at an establishment of her own, however meager. Rowena had appeared more compliant here at Broak than she had at the Cherwoods' home in London, and Mrs. Cherwood began to see the chance of her scheme's realization.

"I'll go this minute!" Greavesey resolved, and without giving Mrs. Cherwood a chance to stop him, make him wait until she could talk with Rowena, he made his bow to her and left.

"Well?" Eliza Ambercot reentered the room when she saw Greavesey leave, and looked inquiringly at Margaret's mother.

"Well!" Mrs. Cherwood said noncommittally. But her smile spoke volumes. "Do you think it would be nice to have a double wedding? Or ought Rowena and that Greavesey to marry first?"

"He asked for her?" Eliza choked.

"Well, not exactly. My niece is her own mistress, you know." Mrs. Cherwood complacently began to fold her silks into her workbasket. "But I imagine he will be doing so in a very short while. It was all very easily managed, my dear."

"But do you think that Miss Cherwood will accept him if he offers for her?" Eliza asked dubiously. "He's so fusty and old, and—"

"But particularly *worthy,* child. I warned my niece what would happen if she didn't take Slyppe when *he* offered. If this Greavesey wants her, I am more than willing to support his suit. And if Rowena has a particle of sense—and whatever else I may say, I believe she is a sensible thing—she will take him. Even if, as you say, he is fusty and old." From her tone Eliza could pardonably have inferred that Mrs. Cherwood was enjoying herself immensely. She was.

"Now, my dear, to that young man of yours." Mrs. Cherwood took up the subject of Lyndon Bradwell as if she had totally settled her niece, and Eliza, liking this topic better than any other, wriggled happily into a chair to listen to her many thoughts on How to Catch a Husband.

"Mr. Greavesey." Rowena spied the man before he found her. She had taken time to change into a day dress of sprigged muslin, to wash the dirt of the garden from her hands, and to repin her hair into a semblance of order. There was a militant glow in her eye and a combatant spring in her step that even her work in the garden had done little to mitigate. Only the general lowness of spirits which had afflicted her since her breakfast with Lyndon Bradwell kept her from enjoying what she regarded as the fray to come. She kept her voice to a civil level and her manner polite, at least for the moment.

"Ah, Miss Cherwood!" Greavesey bowed, his long, pale face flushing with surprise or exertion or excitement—from his demeanor it would have been hard to judge which. "I was just come in search of you."

"How convenient," she said drily. "Have you seen Lady Bradwell?"

"Why, of course. That is why I was sent for, is it not?" His tone managed to be defensive and suggestive at the same time. Rowena, looking away briefly, realized that one of the house-maids was scrubbing in a determinedly unin-terested fashion at one of the brass doorplates nearby.

"Shall we go into the office?" she invited coolly.

Rather meekly Greavesey followed Miss Cherwood back to the office, away from the ears of housemaids. He thought that her manner to-ward him was improved, that she was a little more conciliatory, as well as somewhat subdued since their last interview together. Bearing in mind Mrs. Cherwood's words of encouragement, he determined to speak his heart and mind again, spurred on by what he felt to be Miss Rowena's unlooked-for civility and by the thought of her money.

When the office door closed behind them Row-ena turned again to the doctor's assistant. "How does Lady Bradwell go on today?"

A little startled by what was, given his train of thought, a change in subject, Greavesey re-ported that Lady Bradwell, although a little tired, was in good trim. "In fact, I think that very soon now the doctor will advise that she may abandon her spectacles in all but the brightest light, and go about as she was used to do."

"Well, that's a mercy at least," Rowena mur-mured to herself. "Please sit, sir."

With a florid gesture Greavesey indicated that he only waited for his companion to seat herself. With a sigh Rowena retreated to the chair behind the desk, and Greavesey settled in a huge straight-back chair which dwarfed his narrow frame.

"I had wanted to speak with you, Mr. Greavesey; indeed, I think it is very good that I should have seen you before Lord Bradwell did, for I am certain that he would have done more than simply talk to you." She gave the man such a meaningful glance that he was inspired with a sudden insight: Obviously Miss Cherwood was jealous of his attention to Miss Ambercot in the garden.

"My dear Miss Cherwood," he began, his voice ringing fulsomely over each syllable. "I assure you that I have been much misrepresented in that instance. There was nothing in my manner—nay, in my intentions—"

"Miss Ambercot seemed to feel that there was, and certainly Lord Bradwell did. It's of no matter to me, of course, but I rather thought you would be happy to avoid another facer if Lord Bradwell encounters you; he dislikes to have his fiancée importuned by—well, in any case, importuned," Rowena continued blandly. "I suspect that it would be a very good thing for you if in future Dr. Cribbatt could contrive to make calls at Broak himself, rather than sending you. If you don't care to explain *why* to the doctor, send him to me and I shall make up some sort of Banbury tale which will satisfy him. My point is, Mr. Greavesey, that you are not welcome at Broak, and will become increasingly less welcome when Lord Bradwell and Miss Ambercot are married. Do you understand?"

Certainly Greavesey believed that he understood. Despite her disclaimers, Miss Cherwood cared enough to make a push to protect him from Dr. Cribbatt's wrath. And perhaps did not want him in Miss Ambercot's vicinity for fear that he would be tempted to approach her again.

"Ah, Miss Cherwood, I am overwhelmed by your concern." Rowena regarded him with disbelief. "But you needn't fear that I shall press my presence upon Miss Ambercot. After all, who would attend her when *you* are near? My dear Miss Cherwood, your aunt, a very genteel and kindly lady, has assured me that I may hope, and so I shall not scruple to ask again if you will consider my proposals. I realize that I am not a wealthy man, nor yet a very young one, but I most ardently esteem and admire you, and I am sure that we would go on together very well. You would have your own establishment, and you would no longer be at the mercy of an employer—however kind the employer might be."

Rowena stared at him in absolute amazement. Greavesey, mistakenly encouraged by her silence, continued.

"You are no longer in the—excuse me, but—the first flower of youth; it cannot have escaped you that your chances of marriage must slighten with—again, pray excuse me!—age, and there is much to be said for contracting a marriage with one who so ardently admires and esteems you...." He continued on, oblivious to the look of dawning outrage on Rowena's face.

She was thinking of Lyn's awkward proposal, so earnest and unconsidered that they had finished by laughing. The thought made her heart twist; the pain gave her wrath new fire.

"For mercy's sake, Mr. Greavesey, stop!" She regarded him as levelly as she could. Greavesey, stunned by the force of the interruption, sank back into his great chair, chin waggling emptily. "I have no idea what my *dear* aunt could have told you to make you think that I was more receptive to your offers now than when you last tendered them, but I assure you that I have not changed and I shall not change. I do not see any particular disgrace in growing older; we must all do so, with whatever grace we can manage. As to growing old unmarried, I don't think that is a worse fate than growing old married to a man I cordially detest. I had meant to be as gentle as possible if you even brought the subject up again, but I see that you are impervious to the polite No. I brought you in for no other reason than to inquire after my mistress's health, and to tell you Lord Bradwell's expressed wish that you no longer attend on his mother here. I did *not* bring you here to entertain your proposals of marriage, certainly not proposals couched in terms of insults! Nor shall I ever accept your heart, hand, or any other part of your anatomy, under any circumstances! And if you will not leave now, under your own power,

I shall summon a footman to cast you out bodily."

Greavesey's chin waggled on; he made no sign of removing from his chair.

Miss Cherwood stood and went to the door, calling to the maid at her polishing to summon a footman; then she returned to the room and placed herself against the door as if blocking Greavesey's exit. When a knock sounded she stepped forward, saying to the person who entered: "Would you remove this man, please? He seems incapable of leaving on his own."

"If that is what you wish, Miss Cherwood," Lyndon Bradwell said softly.

Rowena wheeled about to face him, and Greavesey, watching from his startled seat, realized that the focus of Miss Cherwood's wrath had changed, and took advantage of the moment to slip from the room by the garden door.

"It's exactly what I wish, and I hope you do not mean to imply anything else, Mr. Bradwell," Rowena managed to say icily.

"You seem to make a habit of heated discussions with—" Lyn cast a look at Greavesey's empty chair. "Well, he's made his escape now, in any case. But I wonder why the man makes such a determined effort to win you if you give him no encouragement at all."

Rowena choked.

"Lyndon Bradwell, of all the horrible, ham-fisted, stupid—" Words failed her momentarily. "I brought the man in here to find out about your mamma, since I dislike to air your family's business in front of the parlormaids! And to suggest that since your brother is likely to murder him if he catches the man at Broak, he had as well to send the doctor next time, rather than himself. And quite unheralded the man broke into his repulsive protestations—if you please, I am so aged that I had best marry at once, being in imminent danger of dying an apeleader. As to encouraging him, I believe it was my saintly Aunt Doro who egged him on, and were I not a lady—which I begin to doubt—I would happily throw her from the house as well. Now *you* have the gall to accuse me of leading Mr. Greavesey into a Fool's Paradise? Good God! Leaves only for Mrs. Coffee to accuse me of rifling the silver cabinets!"

Miss Cherwood dropped heavily into the chair recently vacated by Greavesey. Above all things she would have liked to burst heartily into tears, but not in front of Lyn Bradwell. Certainly not in front of Lyn Bradwell. Instead she fanned her anger again, turning it into a weapon.

"One thing I must say for Mr. Greavesey, however: He didn't seem oppressed by the notion of my money. It didn't seem at all improbable that I should wish to marry him, even with my *great* wealth." Her voice dripped sarcasm. "Even despite the fact that I had made it very plain to him that I had rather marry a toad. God, I am beginnning to detest men! What a mutton-headed, egocentric—"

"Rowena," Lyn said quietly.

"I don't want to hear it."

"Renna. Sweetheart—" A warm note was in his voice, almost a caress. Rowena fought the temptation to look up and see if the caring tone was reflected in his eyes. No, even if she wanted him to have changed his mind, it couldn't be now, with the bad taste of Greavesey's presence on the hour. "Rowena?"

"I can't listen now. I can't. Even if I wanted to..." she murmured.

"And you don't?" Now Lyn's voice cooled.

"I *can't* listen now. Lyn, I can't tell what I'm feeling. I'm so angry, and so—" Her voice faltered, died away completely. Her head drooped.

Lyn, watching her, wanted for a moment to touch her, hold her, tell her that he was all manner of fools, that he loved her, wanted her, and that his most pressing need at that moment was to take the desperate note of confusion from her voice and banish it forever. But perhaps she was right. This was not the time. He made himself stand away, ignored his own need to touch her; his hand, poised above her dark hair, pulled back.

"Later," he said quietly, and left the room.

Rowena, huddled in the chair, was barely aware of his departure. "I'm just so very tired...." she said sorrowingly to her hands, folded before her face; then, with a shuddering fury, she gave way to her tears.

Chapter 12

"O for heaven's sake, I cannot tell which of you is the more foolish," Lady Bradwell cried disgustedly to her son. "Of all the mutton-headed, straw-witted, ham-fisted clunches I have ever heard of, you take the cake! And as for Rowena! I don't know which of you is the worst. Here I have assumed forever that *Jack* was the stupid one in the family, and you must needs make a mull of your courting like a seventeen-year-old, half mad with calf love!"

"Thank you, Mamma." Lyn bowed ironically. "As a matter of fact, I misdoubt there is anything you can say to me that I have not already said to myself. But if *I* have come to my senses, can you suggest a way to bring Rowena to hers?"

He settled himself dispiritedly at the foot of the lounge and gazed at his mother with a glance as appealing as any he had trained on her when a green boy. For a moment Lady Bradwell was oddly touched, longing to comfort him now as she had that boy, and to assure him that everything would come right in the end.

"Well, have you come to your senses?" she asked at last, gruffly.

"I believe so. I still think it is folly to marry when I have so little to put toward our establishment—I can keep her, but not in the style I should like to do."

"Lyn, my dear, do you think that Renna cares a particle for your style? You know her history, don't you? Think, boy: If Rowena was willing to turn down a very advantageous offer of marriage because she disliked the man who made it—not to mention several other offers I know of when she lived in Brussels with her parents—and was willing to take a place as companion rather than stay with her aunt's family, surely she knows her own mind! And don't you think that you owe her the respect of believing her when she tells you so? No—" She raised a hand to stop all possibility of protest. "Of course you cannot know what Rowena will feel in five years, or even five months. A great deal can happen in a day, let alone a year. Rowena seems to love you, my dear—I shall not argue with her taste, but I sometimes wonder about her good sense. And of all the fustian things to charge her with, a flirtation with Greavesey is certainly the most—"

"I know, ma'am, I know. It was ludicrous, ridiculous, ill advised, and addle-pated in the extreme. And I would still like to plant that funereal bean pole a facer and show him the door, after which I would like to take Mrs. Cherwood and—"

"Now, that is more to the purpose," Lady Bradwell agreed. "We must do something to rid Broak of Margaret's mother, and as soon as possible; else I see very little chance for you to pursue your romance profitably. I wonder if we can contrive to send her back to London and keep Margaret here in Devon? I shall have to think on that." Straightening the disordered fichu on her gown Lady Bradwell fixed her son with a glance of purpose. "Now, I suggest that you go out and shoot at crows or do something, Lyn dear. You never have dealt well with idleness. Any word from Kelvin yet? No? Well, I expect we shall hear something soon. Go ahead now, and if you see Meg or Mr. Ambercot, send them to me."

"Your servant in all things, Mamma." Lyn bowed over her hand with a pretty flourish.

"If it were in *all* things, my dear, we should not be in this stupid fix now. Go ahead." His mother rapped dismissively at his knuckles with her tambour frame.

Margaret Cherwood and Ulysses Ambercot appeared in Lady Bradwell's room an hour later, located finally by Drummey, strolling in the orchard counting green apples and laughing. Drummey, having delivered the summons, returned himself to the house to ruminate on the distressing turn of the young for levity.

"Lady B, you wished to see me? Us?" Margaret shot a conscious look at her betrothed, standing just behind her.

"Come in, children. Close the door." Lady Bradwell waved an impatient hand. "Now, I am about to embroil you in plotting, and Meggy my dear, you are not to take anything I say about—"

"Mamma." Margaret supplied flatly. "I assure you that I have no illusions about Mamma, Lady Bradwell. I must love her, I suppose, but that don't mean I cannot see when she is being impossible."

"Well then, " Lady Bradwell continued, somewhat relieved by this carte blanche. "I think the time has come to return your mamma to London. A lamentably short stay of course, but there are times when things cannot work out just to our satisfaction, can they?" The polite regret in Louisa Bradwell's voice was belied by the gleam of amusement in her eyes.

"If you can get my belle-mamma to return to Town you have my blessings, ma'am, and my fullest cooperation. But how do you prepare to do it?" Ulysses asked.

"Very simply, my dear. I propose to send Margaret and Jane packing off to Wilesby this afternoon. I know that it is still early for you to be traveling, Margaret, but you have mended quite nicely, and I think you can take half an hour in a closed carriage with no great ills attendant."

"I'll go anywhere you wish me to, ma'am, but will that not mean that Mamma will only follow me back to Wilesby?"

Lady Bradwell smiled. "I am very much afraid that I am about to have a relapse," she said softly. "Margaret, has your mamma ever had the scarlet fever?"

"I've no idea, but I can tell you," Margaret's eyes shone with uncharacteristic glee, "Mamma don't like to be around sick people. When my sisters and I were ill she was used to retire to her room with a roast onion, the laudanum bottle, and a box of pastilles which she burned 'til the air was blue, and refused to see any of us until all of us had been sworn healthy by the doctor. I should imagine that scarlet fever would work very nicely indeed."

"Wonderful. Now then, Ulysses, may I ask you to take your sisters and Margaret back to Wilesby at once? You had best tell Anne what we are about—better, send her to me and I will make her part of the plot. And then return to me here? I have further use for you. As for Jack—well, if you see him, explain to him; perhaps he can help, else he'd do as well to join Lyn at shooting. Now, Margaret my dear, if only your mamma will be so obliging as to take her part correctly."

"I think you may depend upon it, Lady B."
Margaret smiled. "But Renna—"

"My dear child, this is mostly for your cousin's
sake! You have Ulysses to take your part. She
hasn't a cavalier. Yet," she added with a slight
smile. "Now, go ahead. We've a great deal to
accomplish here."

Jane Ambercot and Lord Bradwell were located in the stables and apprised of Lady Bradwell's sudden "relapse." Jane smiled evenly:
She had no great affection for Margaret's mother,
who constantly suggested remedies for her
many faults of complexion, figure, and deport-
ment. Lord Bradwell was not as quick as his
fiancée to understand the point of his mother's
plotting, but years of trusting his mamma's
judgment, coupled with a growing dislike of
Dorothea Cherwood, ensured that he fell readily
into the plan. It was he, in fact, who suggested
that he be the instrument to return Margaret
and the Ambercot sisters to Wilesby Hall, leaving Ulysses free to support Lady Bradwell on
the instant. There was a pretty leave-taking
between Margaret and Ulysses; Jane went in
search of her younger sister and returned to the
front hall with Eliza rebelling strongly at this
sudden banishment, and the party set off in one
of the Bradwell carriages.

Dorothea Cherwood had amused herself, since
Greavesey's departure from the garden room,
in discussing courtship strategies with Eliza

Ambercot, and in envisaging Rowena married to Greavesey and Margaret married to Ulysses Ambercot, while cursorily continuing her work on an embroidered chair cover. When Lady Bradwell appeared at the door, a trifle disarranged and rather flushed, Mrs. Cherwood rose with great ceremony to greet her, pleased, inwardly, that she presented a much better appearence than her hostess.

"My dear Lady Bradwell, how do you do?"

"Do?" asked Lady Bradwell vaguely. "O, yes, it's Margaret's mother. How do you do? Dear me, I cannot seem to think straight today. I wish I knew why I feel so distracted."

"Pray do be seated and collect yourself," Mrs. Cherwood offered generously.

"Is it hot in here? No, no, how foolish I am; there is quite a breeze. It is really quite chilly, is it not?" Lady Bradwell fluttered a great handkerchief to no purpose and stared about the room as if it were strange to her. "Have you seen Jack?"

"Jack?" Mrs. Cherwood asked blankly. She had no idea what was the matter with her hostess, but was beginning to feel rather uneasy about sitting so close to her. There was, after all, a breeze in the room....

"My son. Named him after my father. No, it was Lyndon we named after Papa. You haven't seen him, have you? No." She answered before her guest could make a sound. "I rather thought not. He's probably in Naples again. No, that's Lyn. Drat, you'd think I could keep my two boys apart in my mind, wouldn't you? Do you not think it terribly hot in here?"

Mrs. Cherwood stared at Lady Bradwell in amazement. Then began to edge a little away from her.

Lady Bradwell stubbornly moved closer.

"I haven't seen Lord Bradwell," Mrs. Cherwood offered after a minute.

"Why would I want—O, that's right, Jack has the title now, don't he? Dear me, I do feel so queer!" Lady Bradwell continued to fan herself with the huge kerchief, fluttering it now and again in Mrs. Cherwood's direction.

"Perhaps I had ought to ring for something to drink?" Mrs. Cherwood suggested uneasily. "Or perhaps Rowena—yes, certainly, Rowena will know what to do." Whatever her feelings in the past regarding her niece had been, Dorothea Cherwood had a healthy regard for Rowena's ability in the sickroom. "Yes, certainly, I shall desire for Rowena to attend on you, Lady Bradwell."

"Rowena! O yes, the dear child. What a pity she means to leave me," Lady Bradwell murmured. "Well, that is the way of the world. Children grow up and they leave you." Her voice trembled on the edge of tears, then brightened. "I am terribly thirsty. Did you say tea? Or perhaps lemonade. Yes, I think lemonade. We used to have lemonade at the nursery picnics, and—" Lady Bradwell's voice dropped into a murmur, then faded artistically to a sigh.

Mrs. Cherwood rose, purpose in every step,

and rang for a footman. "There now," she said apprehensively, watching her hostess with a distracted eye. "You see, someone will be along directly."

But it was not the footman who entered. It was Mrs. Ambercot, followed closely by Ulysses.

"My dearest Louisa, what are you doing out of bed?" Anne Ambercot fretted. "Lully, you are certain that Dr. Cribbatt has been summoned?" Seemingly she was too taken up in wrapping a shawl about Lady Bradwell's shoulders to acknowledge Mrs. Cherwood's presence.

"He's been summoned right enough, Mamma, but there's word from the village already that the fever is about, and if Lady Bradwell is come down with it again—"

Mrs. Cherwood let out a muffled shriek. "Fever!"

Mrs. Ambercot turned to face the guest for the first time. "My dear Mrs. Cherwood, I beg that you will not alarm yourself. It is only a small chance that the scarlet fever has returned, but I should hate to see Lady Bradwell fall victim to it again." Indeed, Lady Bradwell grew more feverish by the moment, unwrapping the shawl from her shoulders each time Anne Ambercot secured it there, murmuring distractedly that it was *so* hot! "Now Louisa, why don't we take you back to your room, and Taylor will tuck you into bed, and we will fetch you some tea—"

"Lemonade," Lady Bradwell announced defiantly. "I *will* have lemonade. And Mrs.—Margaret's mother, shall come too. Don't you wish some lemonade?"

Mrs. Cherwood blanched.

"Certainly you shall have lemonade," Mrs. Ambercot agreed soothingly, and together with her son contrived to lead the older woman out of the room.

"But—madam, Mrs. Ambercot—" Mrs. Cherwood called after her. "What shall *I* do?" Mrs. Ambercot had passed out of hearing, apparently concentrating upon guiding Lady Bradwell back to her room. Ulysses Ambercot appeared in the doorway for a moment.

"Do, ma'am?" he asked blandly.

"If she's—if Lady Bradwell is truly ill, I really ought not to trespass on her hospitality— it wouldn't be civil at this time, and—"

"In that case, I would suggest that you return to London for a time, ma'am," Lully answered baldly. "Lord Bradwell has already removed my sisters and Margaret to Wilesby House—I hesitate to advise you to remove Meg from there, as she is still not wholly recovered from her accident in the kitchens. And there is always the chance that one of us might have been exposed..." He let his voice trail off suggestively. "As for yourself, I see no reason why you should expose yourself to the sickness, do you?"

Mrs. Cherwood regarded him with positive affection. "No, no, I would only be in the way. You will take care of my Margaret, won't you?" she added in afterthought.

"With all my heart, ma'am." He answered

212

truthfully, repressing an urge to make a caustic comment about his mother-in-law-to-be's maternal instincts.

"Well, then," Mrs. Cherwood mumbled to herself, and set off for her rooms to order out her carriage and set her maid to packing.

And that, Ulysses Ambercot thought with satisfaction, may be the best half-hour's work I have ever done. He turned and went to join Lady Bradwell and his mother in the lady's boudoir.

"She believed me!" Lady Bradwell crowed. "I swear I haven't had this much fun in an age. I should have gone on the stage when I was young. I see it now." The shawls removed, Lady Bradwell and Mrs. Ambercot were regaling themselves with ratafia and laughing over the scene in the garden room. "Ulysses, dear, I beg you will apologize to Margaret if it made her uncomfortable to plot against her mamma in such a fashion. I know it goes against all propriety but—"

"I think everyone rather enjoyed it, Louisa, so stop fretting," Anne Ambercot scolded gently.

"And it has answered famously, ma'am," Ulysses assured her from the doorway. "She's gone off in a pother to desire her maid to pack and her groom to bring the coach round in half an hour. But I recommend that you keep up the charade for an hour or so to be on the safe side. I'll have Taylor alert you when Mrs. Cherwood has actually taken her leave."

"In that case, my dear Anne, I think I am going to have to send you back to Wilesby as well—all for verisimilitude! I shall make your apologies to Rowena, and when Mrs. Cherwood is gone, why, you may all come back to Broak again if you like."

Ulysses cleared his throat consciously. "To tell truth, ma'am, I was rather hoping to show Margaret about Wilesby a bit and—"

"Show her her new home? Well enough, but I want your promise that you will bring her back to visit often."

"Of course, ma'am. I am convinced that Meg would not have it else. You will make our apologies to Rowena, won't you?"

"Good God, Rowena! I hadn't even thought of her," Lady Bradwell whispered. "Goodbye, Anne. Goodbye, Ulysses. And ask Drummey as you go if he can locate Rowena for me?"

Miss Rowena Cherwood, following her disastrous encounter with John Greavesey and Lyndon Bradwell, had uncharacteristically retired to her room to sleep. Now, some hours later, she was awakened by a peremptory knocking on her door, and her aunt's voice demanding admittance.

"Yes, Aunt?" She answered the door, patting distractedly at her tangled hair with one hand.

"This is just to say goodbye, my dear. I cannot stay in a house where there is sickness, Rowena, so do not think to ask it of me. I'm at a delicate time in my life, and it cannot be expected of me, especially for a stranger. Now, I am certain that you will keep an eye on Margaret for me, won't you? Fine. My bags are packed, and although it means I shall have to sleep in a posting house tonight, without my own sheets, too, I shall feel better so. And do consider that Mr. What's-his-name's suit, will you? It may be your very last chance."

All traces of sleep were gone from Rowena's voice. Ignoring the last part of her aunt's message, she demanded: "Who's ill? What are you talking about, Aunt?"

"Your Lady Bradwell, that's who's ill! Came wandering into the garden room where I was sitting, spouting all manner of nonsense, entirely about in her head. Mrs. Ambercot said she thought it might be a relapse of her illness. I cannot stand a sickroom, you know that, Rowena," Mrs. Cherwood insisted querulously. "I am leaving. Write me when things get settled down—I do hope Lady Bradwell don't die of it. And do have that Ulysses Ambercot keep a good watch on Margaret. I *knew* she should have accepted Lord Slyppe."

But Mrs. Cherwood's last few admonitions were spoken to empty air. Rowena, with a sinking heart and clenched teeth, headed quickly for her mistress's room.

She began as she entered—"My dearest ma'am"—only to break off again. Lady Bradwell was seated in her bed, wrapped in a robe trimmed in swansdown and silver, reading the second volume of *Camilla* and drinking tea.

"Drummey found you, dear child?"

"Drummey? No, ma'am. My aunt did, to take her leave of me. And she told me—"

"That I was perishing of the fever, I collect. And half out of my wits as well. Well..." She spread her hands. "I *am* abed, as you can see. And if your *dear* aunt took it into her head to come and take her leave of me, which I place no strong dependence on, I would certainly have a relapse fast enough."

Rowena sat heavily on the edge of the bed, nearly oversetting the tea tray.

"It was all a sham, then?"

"My dear, I simply could not endure her presence here another day, and since I felt that any direct request was likely to cause your aunt to dig in her heels, and to harass you and dear Margaret—who has retired to Wilesby with the Ambercots, by the by—I decided that the time had come for a little mummery."

Rowena regarded her employer respectfully. "My dearest Lady B, I salute you. Obviously I have been taking the wrong tack all these years with Aunt Doro. When I told the truth to her, I would have been better served to have feigned leprosy or smallpox."

"Admit to using rather heroic measures, but it seemed worth it at the time," Lady Bradwell said calmly, sipping her tea. Watching her, Rowena began to chuckle. "That's the thing, my love. I think you need to laugh as much as you need—Lyn, dear! Come in!"

Bradwell stood in his mother's doorway, taking in the scene before him: his mother drinking tea, muffled in swansdown to her chin, and Rowena Cherwood, her hair fallen from its braided crown, laughing weakly to herself.

"You don't seem delirious with fever, Mamma," he said mildly.

"Of course not, darling. Come drink a cup of tea with us."

Rowena moved nervously at the foot of the bed. At the sound of his voice, her laughter had stopped immediately. Now she sat studying her knuckles and wishing fervently that she were elsewhere.

"Perhaps later, Mamma?" Bradwell suggested.

"Now," his mother said with finality. "I have a question to put to you."

Lyn answered with more composure than he felt. "Anything, Mamma."

"Do you love Rowena?"

"Mother!" Bradwell regarded his mother with amazement.

"Lady Bradwell, please," Rowena begged in tones of anguish.

"Do you love Rowena?" Lady Bradwell asked again, and sipped at her tea. "I am past the point of subtleties today, as you may well imagine. I have heard both sides of your stories, and I am tired of waiting for the two of you to make me happy by coming to your senses. Do you love my companion, Lyndon?"

He stood very straight, like a soldier being interviewed on the field. "I do, ma'am."

"Thank you." Lady Bradwell nodded dismissively. "Rowena?"

"Ought I to stand at attention, ma'am?" Miss Cherwood asked irrepressibly.

"No delaying tactics, child; do you love my son?"

"Of course I do, ma'am, but—"

"No buts, please. There now. It has been said, with a most reliable witness. I see no reason why you cannot resolve your difficulties past this point, as you are agreed on the most important matter." As simply as that, Lady Bradwell put down her teacup and raised up her book again. Rowena and Bradwell stared at her for a moment.

Lyn recovered first. "The worst part of Mamma's character is how alarmingly often she is right," he said lightly. "Rowena, you know this isn't how I'd planned to talk to you?"

"I know it isn't how I'd planned to talk to *you*," she admitted.

"Then you will listen now?"

"O Lyn." Forgetting completely where she was, forgetting that her mistress sat not five feet away, Lady Bradwell's companion rose and moved toward him. "I'm sorry for all this brangling to no purpose and—for everything that went wrong. Don't we have more to talk about than our pride?"

"I shouldn't much mind," Mr. Bradwell began, taking Miss Cherwood into his arms, "talking about setting up a nursery, or planning

when we are to be married. But later, I think."
He bent his head to kiss her. "Yes, later."

For a moment the two of them were so involved in each other that Lady Bradwell was able to raise her eyes and admire the sight of them, lost in love and completely unaware of her. With a shake of her head she returned to her book.

"But Lyn, love," Rowena began when she had her breath back. "About my money?"

"What about it?" he asked, smiling. "I was a pompous idiot. If you want to tie it up for the children, sweetheart, that's fine with me. If you want to set up that salon of yours, you have my blessings. For myself, I would prefer to rise in the party according to my own merits, if such a thing is possible in these days—"

"No selling kisses in the street like the Duchess of Devonshire and her sister?" Rowena teased. "Not even one *tiny* little pocket borough?"

"My dearest love, you are enchanting and delightful and wicked and beautiful—and as many other flattering things as I can say. But if I find you kissing tradesmen in the streets, I will *not* be pleased." He ran a caressing finger across her cheek.

"Very well then, I suppose we shall just have to go on as we go on. After all, Lyn, I'm used to making do with a little. Broak has been no challenge at all! At last I can show off my talents as a housekeeper. Did you know I once fed seven hungry marines and their lieutenant, not to mention Mamma and Papa and myself, with one very old and tired chicken! This will be fun!"

Lyn judiciously silenced his betrothed with a kiss. "I'll eat boiled mutton for weeks on end if it makes you happy, darling, but I doubt it will come to that. God, I'm glad we've quit fighting. Another day and I think I would have stormed the office and carried you away by force."

"Which would probably have scared Aunt Doro away as effectively as ever that false fever did." Rowena chuckled into his collar. "And if you hadn't spoken, I imagine I would have simply languished at your door until you came to your senses. That would have been dreadful work, for I'm really very poor at languishing."

"Then I'm glad you were spared it." Another smile, another kiss. "Think," he said a little unsteadily, "of how happy we shall make your aunt!"

"She'll be furious," Rowena disagreed happily. "I believe she wanted me to marry Mr. Greavesey so that she could be certain that I understood the error of my ways in refusing Lord Slyppe's offer. Aunt Doro will be positively livid, and so revoltingly polite that I shan't know how to deal with her."

"Simply feign illness, my love. Or else, we can send her Eliza Ambercot to matchmake for, and that ought to keep them both out of trouble for a time."

"And keep Eliza from importuning you with

her sighings?" Lady Bradwell asked from the bed.

The lovers sprang apart as if shocked.

"Good lord, children, back as you were. You've forgotten about me for this long, I can stand to be ignored for another five minutes or so."

And when Rowena, conscious of her duty as Lady Bradwell's companion, would have broken from Lyn's embrace to plump her pillow or pour out more tea, anything, in fact, to demonstrate her gratitude toward her employer for her generosity, Mr. Bradwell had other ideas. Reaching out with one arm he neatly caught her about the waist and spun her back to face him.

"We've five minutes, sweetheart," he said, kissing her lightly. "And after that..." Another kiss at the corner of her mouth. "After that, we've our entire lives."

"But not in my bed chamber!" Lady Bradwell murmured from the bed. Oddly, no one was listening just now.

CURRENT CREST BESTSELLERS

☐ THE NINJA   24367 $3.50
    by Eric Van Lustbader
    They were merciless assassins, skilled in the ways of love and the
    deadliest of martial arts. An exotic thriller spanning postwar Japan
    and present-day New York.

☐ SHOCKTRAUMA   24387 $3.75
    by Jon Franklin & Alan Doelp
    A factual account of the revolutionary life-saving techniques of Dr.
    R Cowley. The authors investigate the methods, politics and profes-
    sional ethics of Dr. Cowley's controversial medical center.

☐ KANE & ABEL   24376 $3.75
    by Jeffrey Archer
    A saga spanning 60 years, this is the story of two ruthless, powerful
    businessmen whose ultimate confrontation rocks the financial com-
    munity as well as their own lives.

☐ GREEN MONDAY   24400 $3.50
    by Michael M. Thomas
    An all-too-plausible thriller in which the clandestine manipulation
    of world oil prices results in the most fantastic bull market the
    world has ever known.

☐ PRIVATE SECTOR   24368 $2.95
    by Jeff Millar
    Two rival reporters (who happen to be lovers) are onto the same
    story: a game plan of corporate terror and nuclear blackmail that
    threatens the whole country.

Buy them at your local bookstore or use this handy coupon for ordering.

COLUMBIA BOOK SERVICE, CBS Publications
32275 Mally Road, P.O. Box FB, Madison Heights, MI 48071

Please send me the books I have checked above. Orders for less than 5 books
must include 75¢ for the first book and 25¢ for each additional book to cover
postage and handling. Orders for 5 books or more postage is FREE. Send check
or money order only. Allow 3–4 weeks for delivery.

Cost $_____   Name _____

Sales tax*_____   Address _____

Postage_____   City _____

Total $_____   State _____ Zip _____

*The government requires us to collect sales tax in all states except AK, DE,
MT, NH and OR.
Prices and availability subject to change without notice.
8202

GREAT ADVENTURES IN READING

❏ **HERITAGE OF BLACKOAKS**   14424 $2.95
    by Ashley Carter
*A lusty saga of the Old South, where white men reigned supreme
and their women competed with slaves for love.*

❏ **KING OF THE GOLDEN GATE**   14429 $2.95
    by Peter Gentry
*A Barbary Coast adventurer and a beautiful Nob Hill heiress find
themselves in love amid life-threatening danger.*

❏ **GAME BET**   14430 $2.50
    by Stockton Woods
*Cory Williams takes a bet to "shoot" the President with a camera
mounted on a high powered rifle. But he ends up "shooting" a real
assassin and finds himself being hunted as an accomplice.*

❏ **FOUNTAIN OF FIRE**   14425 $2.95
    by Joyce Verrette
*Kidnapped into a Chinese house of pleasure, rescued by the man
she loves, beautiful ballerina Nina Rambovna finds joy and sorrow
across the New World.*

❏ **MAGGIE & DAVID**   14431 $2.50
    by Roger Erickson
*A book for and about young lovers. Maggie, a young lawyer, loves
David and her career. David, does not care about his career in
publishing, but only wants to marry Maggie.*

Buy them at your local bookstore or use this handy coupon for ordering.

COLUMBIA BOOK SERVICE, CBS Publications
32275 Mally Road, P.O. Box FB, Madison Heights, MI 48071

Please send me the books I have checked above. Orders for less than 5 books
must include 75¢ for the first book and 25¢ for each additional book to cover
postage and handling. Orders for 5 books or more postage is FREE. Send check
or money order only. Allow 3–4 weeks for delivery.

Cost $_____	Name _____
Sales tax*_____	Address _____
Postage_____	City _____
Total $_____	State _____ Zip _____

*The government requires us to collect sales tax in all states except AK, DE,
MT, NH and OR.
Prices and availability subject to change without notice.
            8219

NEW FROM POPULAR LIBRARY

☐ **THE SEEDS OF FIRE**   04672 $2.95
by Kenneth M. Cameron
The triumphs and tragedies of the Morse family, a mighty line of
gunmakers, continue in this second volume of the Arms saga.

☐ **THE ENTICERS**   04678 $2.95
by Natasha Peters
While the Chinese revolution brews, four Americans struggle to
find love amid the opulence and savagery of Shanghai during the
thirties.

☐ **FORTUNE'S MISTRESS**   04673 $2.75
by Marilyn Ross
An absorbing historical romance following the life of a young
woman from the dives of London's dead-end streets to the fanciest
salons of Fifth Avenue.

☐ **WHY AM I SO HAPPY?**   04679 $2.95
by Johannes Mario Simmel
A bomb traps seven strangers in the sub-cellar of an old house in
Vienna during the final days of World War II. In their struggle for
survival they come to learn the real meaning of life.

☐ **WILLOWWOOD**   04680 $2.50
by Mollie Hardwick
Lilian seemed the perfect Victorian heroine with her copper hair
and pale, delicate mien. So thought the perverse artist who made
her his model and became obsessed with possessing her.

Buy them at your local bookstore or use this handy coupon for ordering.

COLUMBIA BOOK SERVICE, CBS Publications
32275 Mally Road, P.O. Box FB, Madison Heights, MI 48071

Please send me the books I have checked above. Orders for less than 5 books
must include 75¢ for the first book and 25¢ for each additional book to cover
postage and handling. Orders for 5 books or more postage is FREE. Send check
or money order only. Allow 3–4 weeks for delivery.

Cost $_____	Name _____
Sales tax*_____	Address _____
Postage_____	City _____
Total $_____	State _____ Zip _____

*The government requires us to collect sales tax in all states except AK, DE,
MT, NH and OR.
Prices and availability subject to change without notice.   8217